'Surely one of the best daydream horse
stories written by any hand of the last
decade or so' NAOMI LEWIS

Moon Filly

Elyne Mitchell

Illustrated by Robert Hales

Dragon

Granada Publishing Limited
Published in 1975 by Dragon Books
Frogmore, St Albans, Herts AL2 2NF
Reprinted 1976

First published in Great Britain by Hutchinson
Junior Books Ltd 1968
Copyright © Elyne Mitchell 1968
Illustrations © Hutchinson Junior Books Ltd 1968
Made and printed in Great Britain by
Richard Clay (The Chaucer Press) Ltd
Bungay, Suffolk
Set in Linotype Plantin

This book is sold subject to the condition that it
shall not, by way of trade or otherwise, be lent,
re-sold, hired out or otherwise circulated without
the publisher's prior consent in any form of
binding or cover other than that in which it is
published and without a similar condition
including this condition being imposed on the
subsequent purchaser.
This book is published at a net price and is
supplied subject to the Publishers Association
Standard Conditions of Sale registered under the
Restrictive Trade Practices Act, 1956

For John

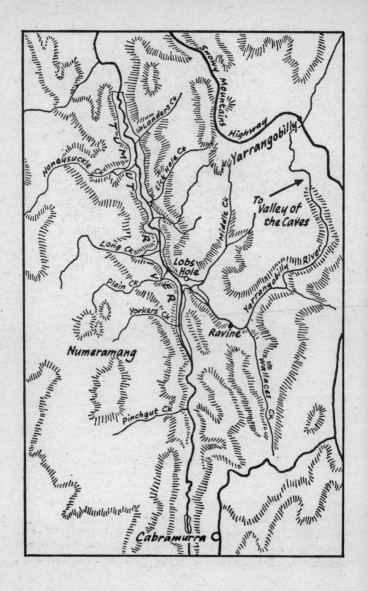

1: *Mare of the Night*

Mares, and foals, and yearlings – they were scattered around the fringes of the big, grassy clearing. They had been half-sleeping in the darkness: now they were suddenly awake, hides prickling. A full moon must have risen behind the huge candlebarks. Something was going to happen. There was

7

light: a magpie carolled. They waited ... tense. Even the foals woke and waited.

The moonlight grew stronger.

Then, in the pool of darkness beneath a great, spreading candlebark, their stallion paced slowly towards them. He stepped out of the shadow, and the moonlight set his mane alight with cold fire. A faint movement, almost a sigh, sounded through the mares. He was back. Behind him were the shadowy shapes of new mares. He was back.

It was the curious young horses, the older foals and yearlings, all less interested in the horse himself, who looked at the mares and foals that followed him. There were two mares close to the stallion – a third lagged behind, and most of the young horses immediately realized that there was something different about her. Exhausted – or ill – as they could see she was, there was something about her, or perhaps not about her so much as a quality that came with her – a past and a future.

She lagged behind and a little filly foal stumbled along at her flank.

One of the colt foals – almost a yearling, but still with his mother because she had no other foal – stood watching for longer than the others did. A light breeze lifted his forelock, ruffled his mane, the forelock and mane that were the same colour of living light that his sire's were, and a strange vibration went through him, a vibration which he had never felt before.

When the mare stopped on the edge of the moonlight and stood breathing heavily, and the little filly folded up and lay at her feet, he could not stop himself from walking slowly out towards them.

The mare took no notice of him and the foal was asleep already. He drew quite close and let his nose drop down to sniff the dark heap that was the very small filly. The little head rose nervously, the ears flicked forward. Moonlight glowed in the eyes, then, as though she realized that she had nothing to fear, she shut her eyes again and slept, but the colt, Wurring, shivered, and he was not cold.

8

He looked curiously at the mare. She was certainly unusual – slender nose and flaring, fine nostrils, fine-boned altogether – but he was too young to know that she must come of some great breed. He looked, and as he looked, she raised her head as though searching the sky. Wurring felt sure something bad had happened to her. Every hair on his body told him this.

He dropped his nose once more to the foal. Once more the eyes opened and the moonlight shone in them. The same shiver went through him, as though snow had fallen on his back. He walked back to the other young horses. His own mother was not far off. Soon he would wander towards her, for after all it was night time, but when he did go to her he realized that she was restless and disturbed. All around the fringe of the flat, mares and young horses were weaving restlessly through moonlight and shadow.

Something had come into their big grassy clearing. Was it the future that had walked in, or was it Death?

None of the herd settled down that night. The moon rose high above the clearing, and the huge, spreading candlebarks threw black shadows. The strange mare only moved to lie down, and she got up again, quite soon, as if she were afraid to sleep on the ground in case she could never stand again. Her foal never moved. Some of the mares realized it looked underfed, perhaps there had been something the matter with that strange mare for a long time – perhaps whatever was distressing her so much was not a recent accident.

As the moon rose, the queer quality of her seemed even greater, and then slowly, slowly, while the silver light faded, she became a shadow: but every horse in the herd knew that she was there.

The young Wurring moved through the herd wondering at their restlessness. Other mares had been brought back before: why, he wondered, was this mare different? He stood in that darkness before dawn, sniffing the air. He listened. What was that old, old mare – the oldest in the herd – neighing to the moonlit sky? That the horse from whom this mare had been stolen would undoubtedly avenge the theft ... this mare came

9

of some special family: sick or hurt though she might be, she was of immense importance.

She was going to die.

As the dawn began to move the darkness, he went forward very quietly and snuffled at the foal again. Once more the foal awoke, and he could feel her eyes on him. He let his nose move over her ears, so gently that he could barely feel the shape of them, but every soft hair transmitted its message ... a thrilling message that was of the future and yet of the past, containing all the mystery of country that he had never seen, the land that had made her bones, the mystery of all the unknown horses whose blood had made her. Wurring felt a flash go through him, and felt as if he were wildly galloping in front of a storm.

The sky grew paler as he stood there. The mare moved once and her head turned towards him.

The foal stirred, unfolded her forelegs, stretched them out in front of her, got up, her ears flickering towards Wurring, her nose quivering. Then she turned to her dam for a drink. The mare nosed her softly, and gave the faintest nicker of pleasure.

Wurring stood quite close, then he saw his sire coming towards them, and even though he had felt a soundless communication – or sympathy – with the mare and foal, and had become vital and strong because of this, he felt small, now, as the huge horse walked towards them. He did not know that he was almost the exact replica of his sire – golden chestnut, pale golden mane and tail, and named for the sun with whose life and light he glowed.

He dared not move, nor stay either ... but it was better to stay. If he walked away he might be more noticeable. Suddenly he felt an unusual gentleness in the big stallion. Even his sire knew that this mare must die: and he certainly knew that she had an immense value.

With great daring, Wurring, the young sun, golden and burning, watched his sire, found himself looking into his eyes for a moment, and saw something he had never seen before – a sadness, a regret, a gentleness. This expression changed as the

10

stallion looked from the foal to his son, but then the horse's attention went back to the mare, and he stood there with her while the sun rose.

As the days went by, the herd's curiosity grew. This mare, who possessed some powerful attraction, was surely dying, and where had she come from? Who owned her? Would there be revenge?

The other two new mares did not know. Winganna had arrived with her, in among their own herd, had taken them with barely a fight, from their own rather younger stallion, and then had brought them all along, rather slowly, through half a day and the moonlit night. The herd all thought of the stallion and three mares and their foals arriving – their stallion who looked like the sun, and a mare who seemed to bring the mystery of the night with her.

Young Wurring galloped with the other young horses, rolled in the snowgrass or on the bare earth, shook till his golden mane and tail flew wild and flashed in the sunlight, ate, and drank the cold mountain water or his mother's milk.

Usually the herd wandered around through the forests and on to other plains, but for sunny day after sunny day Winganna stayed at Numeramang, and there the mare who was the colour of night grazed, or just stood, walked slowly down for water, moved less and less. Each night the moon grew smaller, and it seemed that she grew smaller too.

At last there were only stars in the night sky. At the dark of the moon that mare who was made of the night sky lay down and died.

Wurring saw a shudder, a faint flutter, and then no more movement in the dark shape which was almost invisible on the ground and in the black night. He pressed closer to his mother's flank, his heart pounding in his own chest.

Suddenly there was a queer, echoing neigh, and he could see the little brown foal standing out there in the dark, beside her dead mother, her head thrown up, calling.

Wurring shivered, then he left the warmth and comfort of his mother's side, and walked hesitatingly towards the empty

11

darkness where there was the faint shape of that foal with her head still up, calling, though no sound came.

Step after step, he put down each hard hoof, the dark emptiness pricking at his hide, a cool breeze making him feel every hair, so that for the first time in his life he was completely conscious of his whole chestnut body, from nose and ear tips to rump, from shoulder, back and belly, to hooves – conscious of himself, and nervous.

Young horse, almost a yearling, walking out alone. He had known that death was coming to that mare who had brought beauty and the night to their big grassy space. In fact there was still the same feeling that beauty was present, beauty and some quality of the night that had not been there before she came.

The foal cried out again to the empty night ... and now Wurring walked out to that foal. He walked alone and the foal was alone in the darkness.

He touched the little filly's shoulder, let his nose stray up her mane to her ears, and all the time the electric flashes went through the soft hairs.

At last he turned back to his own dam, not knowing why he had come, or why he was leaving. Then he became aware that the foal was just behind him. Her shoulder was touching his flank as they walked, or sometimes her head. She was very small.

When they were nearly across the empty space he could feel her hesitating: he knew she was placing her hooves down with knees stiff as though she would swing around and go back to her dead mother, and yet her shoulder pressed closer. *He* could not bear to go back. The cool wind, blowing across that space, the piercing shafts of the stars, made him feel too alone and unprotected. He walked on until he reached his dam. His heart was thumping. He had been a horse as he walked towards the dead mare and the foal, now he, himself, was a foal again, and he extended his neck and his nose to suck the comforting milk. Against him he could feel the filly's beating, thundering pulse.

He turned his nose to hers, and then she was gone, suddenly,

12

and he could hardly see the shape of her, out there, trotting, stumbling.

Wurring waited and waited, then he moved out a little into the open, away from the trees, away from his mother, away from the shadowy presence of the other horses.

He stood irresolute – for he was so young, himself, and he did not know what old stories moved in his blood, what forces shook him now, what he would know by the light of the moon, months hence, or what the summer breeze, scented with the blossoms of the mountain ash, would tell him next year.

Out of the night came that high, echoing cry from the foal, and then he could feel her coming back again, straight towards him and she was beside him, pressing her shoulder into his flank.

The two young ones spent the rest of the hours of darkness beside Yarran.

Wurring knew that Winganna, his father, went out through the darkness to farewell the mare. Then, just as the dawn turned the golden stallion into a shaft of sunlight, he led his herd away, and the young Wurring trotted along with his mother. Beside him trotted and stumbled the dark brown filly foal, weak with hunger.

When they stopped to graze, and he drank from his mother, she dropped exhausted. Yarran sniffed at her. Wurring felt that she had lain down. He stopped drinking and nosed her to her feet.

The filly smelt the milk and, on shaking legs, she moved towards Yarran. There was only one foal drinking and Yarran took no notice.

When the herd moved on, the tired foal trotted beside Wurring.

2: *A Brown Shadow*

They spent that night on a little flat where the low-growing, pink and white daisies flowered, and where the surrounding forest was a dark one of black sallee trees, each tree hung with curtains of old-man's beard moss. Not far away there was good grass and water, too, but this was a warm, safe place to camp.

The young horses chased each other among the black sallees. Wurring enjoyed the sensation, half-excitement, half-fear, when the cold ropes of moss slid over his back and rump, or touched his head. He was feeling full of spring ... gay ... mad. It was magnificent to leap away from that black colt who had been faster than any of the other young ones only just before the full moon. Now he, young Wurring, could race away from him through these cold ropes of moss, race him, race him, dig in his sharp hooves, race, feel the leaves and branch-tips whip his shoulders. *He* was the stronger now – he, Wurring.

He stopped for a moment, breathless, to rest and to hide for the fun of hiding, and he was deep in the leaves and streamers of moss. With each deep breath he took in and let out, the moss and leaves moved over his body.

The black colt went past, out of breath too. He had lost the trail. A few other youngsters followed him. Wurring stood while his own pounding blood quietened, and his limbs felt fresh again, fresh to gallop and leap, to twist, to turn, to *dance* as though he were life and the sun itself.

Then there was something creeping into his hiding place from behind ... something ... He turned his head without moving the rest of his body. He had nothing to fear, but who was coming?

There was the little brown filly, half-afraid, half-proud, coming to stand close beside him, heart beating with his, and they shared together the mad excitement of the chase.

Presently Wurring heard the remains of the young mob coming back, and he leapt out of his hiding place and galloped off, setting them a gay chase. Once, when he looked back, he was surprised to see the little filly trailing behind. Then the black colt drew closer. Wurring leapt through some thick trees and almost crashed on to a huge log that was between him and the creek. He braced his muscles and sprang, landing on a loamy bank on the other side of the log. One more jump put

15

him into the creek where he would make no tracks. He turned upstream, and before the creek went round a bend, he pressed into some tea tree so that he could watch the mob come tearing over. Two or three of them fell, and Wurring's knees felt sore as he watched them rap the log. The black colt was well in the lead as they swept down the bed of the creek, with the spray flying.

As Wurring moved upstream, he heard a faint neigh and thought nothing of it. After he had walked a few more yards through the tea tree, he heard it again, and wondered where he had heard a call like that before... and all the time he was wondering he really knew it was the little filly who was calling. It was such a high call. Last time she had cried to the dark of the moon, despairing. Now the call was different: it blended with the last sunset clouds above: it was beautiful and it was partly forlorn. It was also a call to him. He went quietly back.

She was walking towards him. Just then the others all burst into sight, ready to chase him again, and the fact that the funny little filly, who now shared his dam's milk, must have known by instinct which way he went was forgotten.

He did not think then of the flashpoint that had occurred when their hair touched, nor of how it had been impossible to resist going out to them, when the filly foal and her dam had stood alone in the light of the full moon. He just galloped off, leading the other young horses, round and round, in and out of the trees. And often there was the little brown filly catching up, or simply *there*, having taken a wise short cut, there and beside him, her heart's pounding almost shaking her whole frame.

She was beside him when the black colt, Tallara, came at him offering fight. Suddenly it seemed that Tallara thought she was in his way, and he slashed at her angrily with teeth bared.

The teeth only touched her, for Wurring sprang between them and knocked Tallara off balance and then turned on him in the first quite serious fight either colt had ever had. Yet, when they parted, exhausted – and Tallara marked by teeth

16

and hooves – he still rolled the whites of his eyes at the filly, jealous that she should always be with Wurring. Wurring noted with amusement that she paid no attention to Tallara. She was not nervously seeking shelter when she came closer to his hot chestnut hide, she walked with proud carriage, ignoring the black and his bared teeth.

The young horses were all annoyed with her. Wurring was so much the strongest of them all now, and no one could question that he was the leader, yet so often he waited for that motherless filly.

Sometimes they would remember the feeling that went through the herd when the dying mother led the foal into the moonlit flat.

Wurring had named her Ilinga. In truth, of course, this filly may have had a name that no one knew, but Wurring had named her Ilinga, because she had come from far away.

After a few weeks Ilinga did not lag behind so much when they were all galloping. Yarran was mothering her alone, now. Wurring stood close by, but the stranger filly got all the milk, and, though she was still thin, she was growing stronger and taller, and her coat seemed occasionally to have an unusual radiance about it.

The nights grew cold as summer turned to autumn – cold and sharp, then bitter cold, and the white frost lay on the hard ground; furred the grass stems with white. What once had been tall, golden daisies turned to winged seeds on the wind. Bitter cold were the early-falling nights, and the young Wurring stood close to his mother, with the small filly between them.

Winganna became more and more restless as autumn weather stilled the creeks, stilled all growth. Then one frosty morning, when the sun rose bright and clear, sending glittering shafts of light into the bush to touch him with the fire of life, he, a burning, golden horse, led his herd off on one last wild wandering before winter; one last galloping with the wind on the high places, before the snow came.

Wurring wondered sometimes, as they trotted along through

17

mountain-ash forests and on long ridges where the slightest movement of cold air made a quickening of his own identity, whether they might learn anything about where Ilinga and her dam had come from.

They were just where the tall ash merged with snowgums, when they stopped for the night, and the cold wind blew, making both those bright chestnut horses eager, alive, coiled springs of energy, making them dream strange dreams of galloping free on the great, high snowgrass hills before winter came.

Here there was the occasional echoing sound of a neigh. There were no horses to be seen, but Wurring knew they were not far away. . . . He was a horse now: he would go to find them, gallop with them, with his mane and tail flying, perhaps fight a fight or two.

He set off through the trees towards where the last wild neigh had echoed and lingered on the wind – a long, long neigh that shook him with a wild excitement.

Trotting, trotting, he cut across the head of a gully filled with tall mountain ash, and the thrilling scent of eucalyptus leaves that had been bruised by the wind filled his nostrils, the cold wind lifted his mane off his hot neck, thrillingly, thrillingly. . . . Young horse, wildly alive, trotting through the bush.

Behind him, not very close, trotted a small brown shadow, slowly, but keeping him in sight.

Wurring reached the other side of the gully, and a faint track led him up on to a long ridge top where the snowgums grew – white and silver snowgums, wraiths moving in the wind, silver arms weaving, leaves whispering. The track became more defined. He went on, eagerly.

This track turned upwards on a short, thickly timbered spur, and the trees ended. There was a plain studded with rocky tors that loomed like dark islands against the twilight – a high, open plain where the wind sang of life and adventure, where the wind picked up a thrilling neigh and cast it wide, wide over the mountains.

Wurring heard the neigh and saw the scatter of horses in

18

among the rock tors. With more caution, now, he turned off the track and moved around the edge of the plain, watching the other herd. Far over the opposite side, he could see what must be the stallion, a big bay horse, surrounded by mares and foals. Those horses that were spread all over the plain, galloping in the twilight wind, as he wanted to gallop, were younger. He moved out into the open to join them.

The brown shadow, well behind, stopped in the trees, but when the young horses received Wurring with gay galloping and only mock battles, Ilinga went out into the plain too. She moved quietly, but with a swinging stride and a carriage of head and tail that attracted the glances of every horse that saw her.

Wurring was startled when she joined in the galloping, and then, when he saw the interest she stirred in the other herd, he felt an amused pride. Sometimes, when he slowed down, she galloped beside him, flank to flank.

When they stopped to drink at a pool that reflected the last light in the sky, he could feel an excitement throbbing through the mob. . . . These young horses recognized them both as unusual.

The young filly had the bearing of that magnificent breed that had once lived far, far away where the moon rose, and Wurring, who was named for the sun, resembled his sire with forelock and mane the colour of living light.

It was late when Wurring led Ilinga back to their sleeping herd – and she, at least, was tired the next morning, when they all climbed up into the high country, and Winganna set forth to race against winter.

The wind blew cold from the north and cried of snow, and the last golden everlastings bent and rustled in the wind and told a tale of the sun – the last white everlastings whispered of the moon and of the path which moonlight throws across the snow.

19

3: *Legend told by the Falling Snow*

Far, far away, to the east, where both the sun and the moon rise, and where the ground sounds hollow below galloping hooves; where rivers vanish into caverns and tunnels, legend had it, there had once lived a magnificent stallion, and he had stamped some – a very few – of his filly foals with his own unmistakable characteristic, a magnetism as strong as the moon's, the legend said, and with moonlight were they coloured. These mares, in turn, handed on this characteristic to a few of their filly foals. They grew into mares that no stallion ever forgot.

Wurring never knew how this legend came to Numeramang that winter, whether it came in the snowflakes, whether the kangaroos brought it, or the wombats who wandered about, grubbing for food in the daylight, but he knew of it. There was another, equally old legend of a chestnut stallion sometimes being born into the wild herds, a chestnut who burnt with the creative fire of the sun, who blazed with life. Wurring had been named for the sun and though he was still unaware of it, he possessed a quality even his sire had never had to such a degree – the sun's fire.

Now, as the snow fell softly, another legend had come over from the east, and it said that sometime, in some spring of some year, between some day and some night, and in a strange light, the blaze of the sun and the gleam of the moon would meet and blend over bright snow, but before this could happen, the sun would almost go.

These tales were everywhere. Even the lyrebird's dance, deep in the forests, told them, because somehow the legends were as old as the bush and the ancient hills and yet they had been forgotten and were now known again. Now, this winter, the secret of them was called up in the song of the grey thrush, and in the great flight of currawongs, high in a frosty evening sky, that sang and sang of something that was to be, had been and would be for ever, and yet something that was almost impossible – the union of sun and moon.

Winganna had led his herd back to Numeramang just before the first snow fell in the higher mountains. He had been warned by the thrilling cry of the black and white currawongs and the harsh calls of the gang gangs, but he had also known, himself, that snow was coming, known by the colour of the sky, the touch of the wind, and by every hair of his body, every bone, every vein.

At Numeramang, sheltered by the encircling candlebarks, the herd was warm, and though the grass had lost its sweetness, so had every blade of grass in the mountains. Winter was a time for survival, but for the young it was a time to race with the wind and to gallop through curtains of falling snow, a time to learn of great mysteries, a time when their world was made strange and beautiful – and occasionally a time for the impossible to come true.

Ilinga had grown taller, longer legged. Winter had roughened her coat, but Yarran still gave her good milk to make bone and muscle. The very air, laced with snow, made bone and muscle too – and she galloped with Wurring, hooves thundering over bare ground, hooves silent over snow.

After the third or fourth snowfall at Numeramang had fallen and started to melt away, the wild need to wander seemed to enter the yearlings of the herd, and away they went, suddenly, at dawning. Manes and tails caught in the breeze, snow dust flew from their hooves, galloping, wheeling, they vanished through the trees. Ilinga went with them.

This was no short gallop a mile or so from Numeramang and back again. The west wind bore them, urged them, drove them – the west wind blew them to the east. Before mid-morning they were crossing through the Tumut River, breaking ice in the little pools at the edge, pawing at its glassy surface.

Wurring saw his own head reflected in the mirror of ice, saw the forelock and mane ablaze with light. He thought that his father looked at him from the river, and leapt back, but the image persisted in his mind – a horse's head blazing with sunlight.

Half-afraid, he led his followers racing across the cold water and into the bush, but the west wind blew them, and to the east was his desire. In the east, he felt instinctively, lay the answers to many mysteries. Where had Ilinga's dam come from? Why had she died? Why had no stallion come for her? She was not coloured by the moonlight, but there had been something unforgettable about her...yet no stallion had come.

22

On and on they went, straight upwards through rough forest country. At last they reached the top of the immense, forested wall they had been climbing. Only timbered ridges stretched for miles and miles, with a hollow, like that from which they had just climbed, between them and the next ridge. A clear track led north, along the ridge.

Wurring sniffed at it and studied it closely. Every animal seemed to use it, horses, kangaroos, wombats . . . There was even the queer pad mark of an echidna, and this one was very recent. Snow still lay where there was shade.

Wurring turned north along this track, Ilinga close behind him. When he got his breath he started to trot. Speed seemed so important, so wonderful. Soon they would find somewhere where they could gallop. It was also wonderful to be going to new places, places he had never known existed.

After going a little way he could see – and feel – that the valley on the eastern side was opening up. Just then the track turned east too, and he led his little mob down it, slithering on the wet earth, stumbling on rolling stones, steeply down and down.

Then they were on a great open ridge which went tumbling down below them, its lower slopes quite invisible.

Wurring raised his head and looked across the valley. His ears pricked forward. There were rock cliffs – a queer, plum-coloured rock – a lace of waterfall coming out of one sharp cut valley, and steep slope after steep slope falling into the valley.

Their track skirted around a cliff that was the same colour as the ones opposite. Even the soil was plum-coloured, and in places snow still lay.

The mob of young horses slid their way down. At one particularly steep place they paused to look and listen again.

Up from below came a long, eerie neigh.

There were horses down in the valley. Wurring did not move for a moment, but before he had time to feel afraid, that neigh sounded again.

Why should he fear, even if all escape routes lay upwards? He started down again, feeling filled with curiosity, and his

23

curiosity was deepened by the sight of Ilinga, whose expression had become strange, as though a memory had stirred . . .

He went down the last part of the drop, off the track, hidden in a gully, but he had already seen quite a lot of the valley floor. Only a few horses were in sight, and there were some things of odd shapes, things, not horses nor any animal. For a horse as young as Wurring there was nothing much to fear. In any case, stallions do not fight very much in mid-winter when the cold, and the snow, and the lack of food are their enemies.

Wurring walked quietly out into the deep valley.

Only those few horses . . . and no others appeared out of trees and scrub. Wurring looked at them before he studied the queer-shaped things.

Only one of the small mob took any notice of them, and this one was an older mare, a grey with a big foal at foot. She came up and had a good look, a long look, at Ilinga. Then she looked curiously at Wurring.

He failed to find out what she was so curious about, but later he heard her forlorn-sounding neighing, and she seemed to tell the wind, and the cliffs, and the stream that ran down the valley, seemed to cry to the grass and the trees: 'Lost, all is lost except courage. There is evil to come, and great danger, from far, far away. Old tales may come true, true . . .' Her sad neighs died down, and the echoes slowly faded around the cliffs.

Wurring went to inspect the squares of mud and the high rocks built up like a tree. He could not know that this was a building in which men had lived when there was a copper mine at Ravine, but he did not like the feeling they gave him. He looked at Ilinga to see if they brought her any memories. Her expression was still the same, puzzled, alert, as though something she had once seen were being half-disclosed again.

Down at the creek there was an open flat, enough space for galloping. Wurring began to play, buck, rear, gallop round and round and soon the other young ones were following him with mad joy. In what strange future would they be taking part? Was not every future that was worth anything, strange and

24

unknown? But were these young horses enfolded in something compelling that had been foretold centuries before and written in the line of flight of the birds, told in the rhythm of the kangaroos, told in the dance of the lyrebirds and the brolgas? Was there something foretold and so compelling that they sought its fulfilment, sought the answers to their questions, sought the unbelievable fire and joy of the sun and the mystery of the moon with every muscle, every sense they possessed, with their eyes, their ears, and the vibrant hairs of their bodies?

Ilinga, with rough, dark coat, moved with such wild joy that suddenly it was necessary to make the whole of Ravine ring with their neighs, so that their happiness challenged the world.

Wurring could feel the way in which the other horses joined in – a sort of throb of excitement going through his young mob, as if they all knew that the future held great dangers, high magnificence.

The grey mare stood and watched them, the other few horses watched too, watched the sunlight flaring on Wurring's coat, even though it was winter-thick, flaring in his tossed mane, his streamer tail.

First the grey foal galloped to join them, then the others, and last of all the mare, and they danced a dance to call down joy from the winter sky, and strength, and wisdom, and courage: and it also called for beauty, and for mystery from the earth and from the night that must come – glory from the stars and the moon. Glory, yes glory.

Then suddenly Wurring was galloping down the stream, along the clearing, then threading through timber, galloping and jumping, keeping on and on till the bush opened on to another small flat. The horses burst through the trees on to this flat, across it, and into the water.

They were at a junction where two streams met – deep pool and shallow bar, then the swift-rippling, wide waters of the Tumut.

A junction, a meeting. Why was the whole bright day filled

with an ancient meaning that had been known in the past and was still to come true?

It was hot, and they drank at the meeting place of the waters. Strong, cold water tugged at their legs, while the slippery stones rolled under their hooves, and the waters told Wurring: 'Further east, further east. Not now, the time will come.'

The birds, flying overhead, were crying of snow.

Numeramang was sheltered when snow fell. They thought of Numeramang, and with the thought they were away, the wild young horses, racing for home – racing the winter, and racing the snow: racing Time, so that the age-old words whispered by the grass and the trees, told in the movement of the snow crystals and the music of the wind, must come true.

4: *A Dance of Winter, a Death in Summer*

Snow, snow, snow, the flakes came drifting down, drifting, whispering. The loads of snow might slip from the smooth, leathery leaf or silver branch, and whisper as it fell softly into snow on the ground. A snow crystal, star-shaped, glittering points, might land on the fur tips of Wurring's ear and transmit its message that the world was wonderful, and his, if he earned it. The whole rhythm of the moon, the grace of sunbeam, the blazing fire without which nothing can live – his, if he earned them.

Snow crystals fell on Ilinga, jewelled her ears, nose, mane, back.

There was still grass close below the light covering of snow. Winganna would not move the herd lower down unless the snow became heavier.

It was still possible to gallop. By day the snow-spray followed behind like a cloud: by night, when the young horses went madly tearing round, the spray was The Milky Way.

Then the winter did get heavier, and the old stallion led all his herd lower, into forest country where the grass was rather hard to find, but where they were warm, and could find at least a little food without having to dig for it.

The young ones roamed for miles and miles in the forest. Sometimes the snow even fell down there, white flowers on the unflowering ferns, a winter blossom on the tall peppermints. Once Wurring and Ilinga, alone, went deep into a damp gully that was filled with blanketwoods and great tree ferns. There was a small flat floor to the gully – not just the hillsides dropping steeply into a narrow creek.

27

The two young horses paused for some reason, as they were about to put their noses to the freezing water and drink, and they stood perfectly still among the snow-touched ferns.

There was a lyrebird dancing his dance to the snow, tail outspread.

Wurring and Ilinga watched the dark bird's steps, the miming, the movement of the delicate, beautiful tail. There, in the cold, snowy gully deep in the bush, they watched while a lyrebird danced and the snowflakes, which are made by the music of the spheres, fell slowly through the freezing air.

Many mysteries can be woven into a dance and a rhythm to the music of falling flakes, to the soft whisper of snow, but it is not always easy to understand, even while the perfect movements are danced.

Wurring and Ilinga watched, standing absolutely still.

The lyrebird might have known that he had re-discovered a dance which told an old, old legend of the bush, he might have known that his dance told of the sun and the moon – of a strange night and a strange light over snow. Wurring felt this in his bones and veins, but it was not something that he could *know*, like he knew that sweet grass would surely grow at Numeramang in the spring.

Colt and filly, they watched till the lyrebird had danced all the mysteries of the world, and had vanished into his dark thickets.

Then they heard a dingo crying as though he were crying to the moon.... Or was it a dingo? Was it that lyrebird just teasing? Then suddenly there was a sound like the far-off cry of an angry stallion. Wurring shook the snow out of his mane. That lyrebird *must* have seen them. He started back to the rest of the herd, Ilinga close on his heels.

* * *

Winganna took the herd to several haunts he had visited in other winters, and where he knew there would be shrubs and grass to eat. At last warm weather came, and the snows were melting into the streams. It was time to go back to Numeramang, to climb up and up, and finally go through that ghostly black sallee forest, then through their own candlebarks into the big clearing.

The grass was free of snow and beginning to show some life.

The heap of bones that had once been that dark mare had been dispersed by dingos. Nothing now really told the exact place where she had died, but both chestnut horses, sire and son, knew where it was.

Yarran's milk had stopped by the end of the winter, for she was in foal again, but Ilinga was well grown, and no longer needed it. She still shadowed Wurring, and the other colts had become increasingly jealous about it.

The grass grew fresher, sweeter every day. Strength seemed to surge through the brumbies, through the kangaroos, the wombats, all the wild animals. Then, one day as the sunlight sparkled into the plain, spring was suddenly there, and Wurring was indeed a horse, golden, burning, a shaft from the sun. Now it would be the fillies, too, who snapped and kicked at Ilinga, to chase her away from her foster brother, the horse who was the sun, but Ilinga walked with pride beside him.

Once, early that spring, they were contentedly grazing, when Wurring felt a prickling of danger in his coat. Just at that moment Winganna must have felt it too, because he flew, with tremendous fury, into a thick clump of scrub, and apparently chased another stallion. Wurring followed, but he did not get more than a glimpse of an iron-grey horse – who was heavy but could gallop – and, after a while, being not yet a two year old, he could not follow the mad chase any longer, and had to stop and stand, feet spread, head down, gasping for breath, and the sweat dripping off him.

Who was the horse who had been watching them?

A wind blew out of the east, and touched his hot coat.

Wurring found Ilinga as he went back – knew he would find her because of the strong feeling of her presence well before he saw her – and, as he looked, it was as though he saw her for the first time. She was different, beautiful, and, because she was beautiful, danger had come into their lives.

They went back together, and had been with the herd a long time before Winganna returned.

The huge chestnut was very tired, they could all see this, and he walked towards Ilinga and looked at her earnestly be-

30

fore he went off to roll in his rolling hole to get the sweat out of his coat.

After all, what is danger? What is pain?

Only Yarran, whose son was so handsome, and who had fostered the filly from far away – the filly who was now becoming so beautiful – only Yarran knew that danger was indeed danger, for both the young and for those who are losing their swiftness, as Winganna was losing his.

The grass grew and the pea bushes blazed with gold and brown peas – gold for the young horse, velvet-brown for the filly. They galloped, they leapt, they rolled in the sun, growing stronger every warm, sunny day, and Wurring was wild with the joy of life.

What was danger?

He led the young mob of colts, and also the fillies who followed him, galloping over the mountains, but they could not really get far because the rivers were very high, full of the water from the melting snows.

The young horses grew stronger, but that long hard chase must have strained Winganna, because he took a long time to gain the full glory of his summer coat and regain his vigour.

Yarran wondered if that other horse would appear again. If he were far younger than Winganna, he too would be strengthening with each warm day.

Then one evening a flight of black cockatoos flew over Numeramang. The weather was clear, and it was most unusual for black cockatoos to utter their weird, wild calls in fine weather, but this evening their crying could be heard for a long time before they appeared. It was of winter and death that they were calling, on this lovely summer evening.

The rivers had dropped sufficiently.

He came two nights later, his dark, iron-grey hide almost invisible in the night. Clouds seemed to come with him.

Some of the mares smelt him before Winganna did, because, when he started threading his way through the herd, he kept well to windward of the stallion. At last, either he could not find what he was looking for, or he determined to attack,

31

for he gave a roar, and, with a mighty rush, he sprang for the chestnut.

Winganna was taken by surprise, and the other horse, with his dark colour, was less easy to see than he was, himself.

Wurring heard the roar, heard his sire's answer, and he felt the hair along his back standing up. Then, as he drew closer to the rest of the herd, he could feel terror running through it, like a fire, from horse to horse.

Terror ran wild that night, for those two stallions fought throughout the darkness, hour after hour; drawing back, resting, and then starting again. All night long there was the smell of blood and churned-up earth, and sweat. There was the sound of pounding hooves, the gasping, rasping breaths, and sometimes a scream rang out to the stars.

The watching herd could only see the vast, struggling bulk of the two horses fighting for their lives – a rearing shape, for a moment, head and forelegs and huge shape of chest and upstanding body suggested against the night sky, the flung mane, the straining haunches.

Even like that, a silhouette against a lighter cloud, they could tell the greatness and nobility of Winganna – their stallion. The other horse was heavier, not ugly, but with a sort of horrifying characteristic that seemed to show in every movement and certainty emanated with the smell of him. This characteristic, this odour, was of cruelty.

Thunder of hooves on the ground, the dull sound of hooves on flesh, the flash of the whites of the eyes, flash of teeth, the stench of blood, of sweat, and the rasping heave of their breathing – the night contained this and nothing else. It all added up to horror and fear.

Wurring heard and smelt it all. Yarran heard and smelt too, and knew that it was this of which the black cockatoos had cried: 'Winter and death.' Ilinga, standing beside Wurring, was shaking all over with a terror that was far greater than any of the others seemed to feel.

Wurring should have taken her away, but he could not know what the outcome of this battle would be – the two stallions

32

seemed to be so evenly matched – and there was the dreadful attraction of the fight. He did not know who the cruel stallion was, did not know that he was years younger than Winganna.

Being equally matched would not give Winganna victory. Only luck could do this: the other horse, unless he was unlucky, would endure longer.

Luck came for Winganna once, but it was not sufficient. The cruel iron-grey horse slipped, and for a second his quarters and flanks touched the ground. Winganna was too tired to move fast enough, and the other was up before he could leap on top of him and beat him down.

Slowly, through the dark and clouded hours, Winganna was worn down, and, at last, finished.

Yarran shook all over with fear. This sun, Winganna, her mate, was dead and the next one, possessor of more of the sun's fire, was Wurring. Would the iron-grey horse realize this and maim Wurring, as she feared he might? They should go, but somehow they could not leave, and it might, indeed, be death to move.

The dawn came, and the strange stallion had something else on his mind. He started immediately to race through the herd, searching for something. When he did not find it, he tore all around the flat, looking among the trees. Then he came back to the herd, and it was clear that he was full of a desperate fury. Whatever, or whomever, he was seeking was not to be found.

Then he rushed among the young horses and the mares, kicking and biting indiscriminately. Wurring was knocked sideways with a savage blow. The horse, in an uncontrolled fury, raged on.

Before Wurring could pick himself up and collect the thoughts in his spinning head, the horse had stopped in front of Ilinga.

Ilinga was terrified, mesmerized, as though watching a snake. At last she started to move backwards. The horse stared and stared at her. Slowly, slowly he began to move forwards. Just then Wurring's head stopped spinning, and he sprang, but the horse shook him off without seeming to notice him.

33

Ilinga turned, with a scream, to gallop away. Any doubt the horse might have had about whether she was the daughter of the mare for whom he was searching, went when he saw her moving. She moved with the rhythm that only mares of a certain breed possessed. He shot forward after her. Wurring sprang forward too.

It was lucky for Wurring that the blow he got on the head knocked him unconscious without seriously injuring him. Otherwise he might easily have gone to his death, following the stallion who was now driving Ilinga away – to the east.

The watching herd were all shaking with fear. This was something that had been foretold, but all the other wild animals of the mountains had known it better than they – the animals like the kangaroos and the wallabies who had really been forever and forever of this earth, air and water. The grass, the trees, the wind, and the snow, itself, had known that this was going to happen, and had cried it aloud for those who had ears to hear. Other things had been cried aloud too, but now the whisper in the leaves' singing was: 'Danger! Danger!'

5: *Brolga's Warning*

Wurring felt as though he were at the bottom of a dark hole, fighting to stand, fighting to be still, fighting ... something. The hole was going round and round. There was light far away. Then the light whirled closer, whirling, bigger, bigger. If only he could be still. Bigger and bigger, the light was rushing towards him. He seemed to see Yarran's head. Then he shut his eyes, and there was nothing. After a while he could feel the cool earth beneath him: the cool earth and it was still. When he raised his head all the surrounding forest started to spin, and in the still centre of the sky was Ilinga ... but this was a dream. Ilinga was only in his head, for she was not really there.

It was two days before Wurring could do more than reel giddily to the stream to drink.

After those two days no scent hung to tell him where the iron-grey had taken Ilinga.

Most of Winganna's herd had vanished. Only Yarran remained, and three of the fillies who had been most jealous of Ilinga, one having come as a foal when Ilinga came.

Wurring was grateful for their company, but as soon as he could really move, he must find Ilinga, must search the bush and the great high plains where snow would fall in winter, search, search, search. To the east he should go ... surely to the east.

At last he could jog along without his head spinning so much that he fell, so he started off on the track they had taken for Ravine. Yarran and the fillies following. Down by the Tumut they found some of Winganna's herd, and Yarran, soon to foal, stayed there with them. Wurring led the fillies steeply up the hill, the same way as he had gone before.

35

When he reached the top he felt an irrational hope that he would find Ilinga waiting for him, down there, where they had played together. The moon was risen...and it was by the light of the moon that he had first seen her....

He led on down the slope, picking a way where they could be as quiet as possible, but it was so steep that they slid often,

36

bumping shoulders and flanks against the rough-barked peppermints, or occasionally against a white ribbongum. The cliffs on the opposite side were in shadow and looked dark and threatening because of the moonlight elsewhere. Wurring felt that the sound of their slithering must echo off those cliffs and fill the whole valley. He was glad when they could enter into the gully down which he had gone the last few hundred feet, that other time he went down. He stood and waited for a while so that any noise they had made might be forgotten.

Then, as they waited, a sound filled the air. Wurring felt the hot, sweaty hair stand up all along his back. The fillies crept close. The rough trumpeting grew louder. He looked up. Great wings were passing over the moon.

Wurring recognized the sound, saw the enormous birds, but, even though he realized what they were, his heart kept thundering in his chest. The brolgas were circling: there was nothing to fear; yet what news did they bring? Black cockatoos had told of the winter of Winganna and his death. The lyrebird's dance had mimed a story ... a story whose truth he could only feel, not understand. What did this flight of brolgas mean? What did the shadow of those great wings across the moon portend?

Under cover of their trumpeting, he led the fillies down and down the narrow gully. The hair still stood up on his back, the skin still crept, his heart still pounded.

The brolgas, calling continually, began to circle lower and lower. They were enclosed within the cliffs, making ever smaller circles within those walls, and their calls echoed, echoed, echoed, till the whole of Ravine was filled with the weird clamour.

Added to this noise was now the sound of thundering hooves, for a brumby herd was galloping downstream as the brolgas landed on the grassy flat by the creek. Wurring and the fillies stood among a few trees, tense, frightened, but watching.

The birds landed and arranged themselves in the pattern of a dance, folding and unfolding their wings, the soft grey feathers silvered by moonlight, the red heads dark. There were

37

three pairs, advancing, bowing, retreating, picking up sticks, throwing them, catching them. Then suddenly the usual pattern altered, the wings were unfolded more often, catching the moonlight. The birds mimed danger and fear, mimed wounding and recovery ... danger and fear, above all, danger. Then slowly they seemed to dance no longer to each other but to the moon, the moon alone. And then when they were done, they ran with wings outstretched again and took off down the valley, circled upwards and upwards, as though drawn by the magnetic pull of the moon, great wings blotting out the silver light, calling, calling, till they were at an immense height. At last, one by one, they flew off towards the east.

Danger, danger. Wurring felt that every call told him danger. To the east lay danger – but to the east lay the only way which Ilinga would have gone.

First he would very quietly follow that frightened herd. From the sound, it was quite a size – contained more horses than had been here on his previous visit. From them he might learn something. But when he drew close to them, where they stood, still nervous, far down past some of the mud brick ruins, he could see that there was a mature, heavy bay stallion. Clearly it would be foolish to go too near. It was just as he stood, hidden in some bushes, watching, that a furious neigh, a stallion's neigh, rang out from high above on the eastern side of the valley.

*   *   *

Ilinga had been given no chance to stop, by that furious, iron-grey stallion, until they reached the Tumut River, about midday on the day after he had killed Winganna. He had to stop to drink there. She needed water too, but even her thirst could wait if she could escape while he drank.

She waited till he must have been very full of water – brown filly standing in the rippling silver stream – then braced herself, swung round, and leapt away: but it was as though that horse felt the first bracing of her muscles, because he had got

38

round her, before she had got to the first line of trees, and was threatening her with bared teeth.

He drove her back into the water and made her stand in front of him, while he finished drinking.

Ilinga shivered with terror and misery, and the icy touch of the water. She watched the horse fearfully. It had been obvious that he had thought he recognized *her*, after he had failed to find whatever it was that he sought in the herd, but she could not remember ever seeing him. She had indeed felt a flash of fear and loathing when she smelt him, before he leapt at Winganna. Then, as she stood shivering in the middle of the Tumut River, she wondered if this horse could have been the one who had stolen her mother – and hurt her – for this was a violent-tempered horse. Something or someone had hurt her mother, she was sure, before ever Winganna came and took her from . . . from whom? Ilinga looked closely at the iron-grey, but she could not remember. The horse began to move towards her. His ears were layed back and she hated the look of him. She spun round, lashing out with her heels.

He struck her heavily on the quarters.

A shrill squeal of anger and surprise was forced from her. It was certainly not worth being lamed by this horrible horse. She moved on, wondering why he had singled her out, whether he had owned her mother. She wondered suddenly if this could be her own sire, and almost stopped in her tracks, but got a swift bite. She looked around with loathing, lashed out and sprang aside, so that the heavy blow missed her.

What was it that had been in the thrush's song? 'A filly coloured by moonlight, like the moonlight mares used to be coloured of old, a filly sired by the night wind, begotten on a mare of the breed of the moon.' She knew she was not coloured by moonlight, only a very dark brown.

The iron-grey was too heavy to go fast up the hill out of the Tumut. A heavy, loutish horse, no sire of hers, she was sure. Twice when she tried to break away, he bit or struck. Perhaps he would get more tired, after all he had been fighting all night. She went faster. She would go the way he wanted, but she would make him travel faster, try to wear him out completely, and then get away.

Soon he was blowing and sweating, but fear had made her tired too, and her own heart was thumping. She could not do it, could not go fast enough to get away. She strained on upwards through the bush, tiring herself while she tired the horse.

When she turned along the track that Wurring and she had taken into Ravine, he swung her southwards so that they would go round the head of the valley. She realized that this was country she had never been in before. When Winganna brought her with her dam to Numeramang, he must have brought them through Ravine for it to give her that feeling of recognition. Soon the iron-grey turned her in a more northerly direction, and when they had gone some distance, they struck a track which went east. Once they were going along this track, she again got that indefinable feeling that she knew the country. She must be going back where she had come from.

She tried to husband her strength so that on the next steep hill she might beat him, but no steep hill came for a long time, they just went on and on; and though that iron-grey seemed almost exhausted, so was she. At last he stopped. He had picked his resting place very cunningly. He stopped in a small, sheltering clump of snowgums in the centre of an open plain. Which ever way Ilinga tried to escape, she would have to cross open country.

She felt certain that if she were to escape at all, she must do it before they reached his usual grazing ground, the place where his herd ran, and before he became rested. She looked at him standing with his head drooped, the thick olive-green leaves of the snowgums all around him. He was so strongly built that it would take more than a night's tremendous fighting and a day's travelling to exhaust his reserves.

He raised his head and looked at her, and she knew that his mood was still evil. He would do anything to stop her getting back to Wurring. Anger seethed inside her, but she stood quite still, and let her own head droop with an exhaustion that was not all feigned.

40

Slowly night seeped over the plain. Ilinga pretended to sleep – and, since she was very tired, slept fitfully – but she kept looking through her eyelashes at the horse. He slept, and, as the night grew darker, he slept very heavily. Ilinga knew this by his breathing and the relaxation of his solid body, even his ears.

She stepped silently sideways – as though moving to an unheard music, gracefully, silently stepping to the side – sliding away from the stallion, out through the silver-limbed trees into the dark night before the rise of the moon.

She was shaking all over, and it was difficult not to turn and gallop for her life. Controlling herself, she walked away, placing each hoof with desperate care, and she went northward, rather than directly towards where Wurring would be.

The stallion would roar, if he woke and found her gone. She would have that as a warning. On she went, slow-placed feet on clumps of snowgrass, barely allowing herself to breathe, ears straining back to hear if he moved, eyes straining forward, trying to pick the best line to go across the open plains, her coat iced-over by fear and by the cold south breeze.

The dark line of trees grew closer, closer. Holding her breath, she entered into them.

Was she far enough away, now, for the sound of a stick cracking under her hoof not to carry back to him? She did not know. She must creep still, allow no branch to swish off her shoulder or rump, tread on no stick or stone. There must not be a sound. When he woke he must not know which way she had gone.

The trees were quite thick and it was difficult to be quiet. If only they would open out a little, she would be able to trot. Slowly radiance began to filter into the woods. The moon had risen. Time had passed. A narrow glade opened ahead of her. She cantered, soft-hooved down the snowgrass, every step taking her further and further from the iron-grey.

She would keep going north for a little while longer and then try to make her way west again. She hoped she could find a way through country that was not too thickly timbered and

41

not so open that she would be visible for all to see. She kept listening – listening acutely – feeling with every hair for the moment she was followed.

The only animals that saw her were a few wombats and a dingo that stood in deep shadow. She glanced sideways at the strong, yellow dog and knew that she had nothing to fear from him. She was strong and free, like himself. The dingo watched and saw a dark brown filly trotting gracefully through moonbar and shadow, not with pride in her movements but with a certain quality of magic – a quality of having been forever and yet ever renewed.

Ilinga went on and on through the night and no sound of a searching iron-grey came to her. At last, when she was so tired that she felt she could go no further, she found a very dense thicket of snowgums and wriggled herself into the centre of it where there was just enough space to lie. She slept for many of the daylight hours.

It was thirst and hunger that woke her. Before moving she listened carefully for quite a long while, then she got out of the thicket as silently as possible and went in search of grass and water. She spent the rest of the daylight grazing and drinking.

Once she set forth on her journey again, she went slowly and carefully west, but she was still far further north than the course on which the iron-grey had brought her, or even than a line that would take her directly into Ravine. In all the hours of the night there was no sound to worry her. She saw some wallabies and many wombats. Once there was a small herd of horses. They neither saw her, nor smelt her, and she pressed on, with beating heart.

Presently she began to circle a little southwards. She must be getting near Ravine, near to where the Lobbs Hole creek ran into the Tumut. She intended to drop into Lobbs Hole, cross the creek, work her way upstream through fairly thick scrub, into Ravine, and then quickly up the other side. Somehow she never thought of Wurring being anywhere else but Numeramang.

As she crept up to Ravine she saw a large herd of horses. There was no horse, filly or colt that she knew among them all, and the stallion looked strong. Even from some distance off, she felt the extraordinarily powerful sensation of fear and danger coming from them. Something had happened not long before.

6: *Danger, Danger*

Wurring heard that furious stallion roar and his heart jolted
and sent the blood pounding through him so that he was shaking all over.

It was the sound of the iron-grey, and Ilinga might be with him.

The roar rang out again, from somewhere above. Wurring began to creep towards the sound, keeping out of the moonlight. The fillies were following him, and when the roar sounded again, he forced them to stay back, then went on very carefully himself.

That iron-grey was making no effort to be quiet. He started to crash down the hillside, screaming his rage.

It was not till it was too late that Wurring realized that the crescendo of screaming had been caused by a warm current of air taking his scent upwards, straight to the stallion above him.

In a few terrible moments of noise, and dust rising against the moonlight, that horse had found Wurring and then the fillies, and apparently realized that Ilinga was not in Ravine, so that he turned on Wurring, in a tearing rage.

Then Wurring knew the brolgas' cry of 'danger' was absolutely true. Blows began to flail around him. He tried to fight. The horse was twice his weight and twice his age – and Wurring had had no experience of real fighting.

He was knocked over, he was pounded, he was kicked, and when he got on his feet, he was driven up the hill, just as Ilinga had been driven, with no chance of escape.

This time the horse was not tired, and he drove Wurring fast up hill and fast over the flat, fast along the ridge tops, and fast down into the valleys.

Wurring was aching all over from the blows he had received, but slowly his brain began to work. It was obvious that the horse had lost Ilinga and that he was being taken instead, probably he might be used to attract Ilinga back.

If Ilinga had escaped from the iron-grey, it would be doubly hard for him, the second one, to escape, but he would have to try to do it – and quickly. He thought that the only way for him to get away would be by going fast. Surely this horse was too heavy really to gallop fast.

Wurring did not know that he, himself, was too young to go fast for very long. He learnt this, and learnt it very painfully,

45

when he tried to gallop away, in a long, gently rising, snow-grass glade. His take off and speed gave him a start, but the older stallion caught him in a very few minutes, or even seconds, and leapt in front of him, striking him till he stopped.

Wurring, when his head had cleared, wondered how Ilinga had escaped.

He knew then that, if he were to remain alive, it would be better to keep going in front of this evil-tempered horse. Already one shoulder was so hurt that he found it increasingly difficult to move fast. It was also difficult not to get so angry that he risked all and turned to face this iron-grey tormenter, the killer of his own sire. However Wurring knew, as the moon sank, and the night faded into day, that he must stay alive and grow old enough and strong enough to kill this horse, avenge his father, and remove the danger to Ilinga.

As they trotted on and on, they passed quite a few young horses. Wurring noticed that these usually galloped off. This was not to be wondered at. This iron-grey horse with the red, flaring nostrils and always the whites showing in his eyes, this horse with his ugly, thundering body, was enough to cause fear and hatred in any younger horse.

Wurring had no real fear – not then. He still felt so strong in his youth. He went on, giving no trouble.

They left the trees behind, and were on great, rolling, empty snowgrass hills and plains. A river wandered around the ridge ends. There were enormous collections of rocks piled one upon another. The sky was starting to cloud over a little, and a cold wind wailed among the rocks. The loops of the river grew steely grey.

Wurring's shoulder was becoming very sore, but there was no possibility of being able to stop. He kept going, and his natural pride showed in every line of his beautiful chestnut body – kept the fury ablaze in that iron-grey stallion.

On these open hills they saw no horses. As they went steadily eastward Wurring began to remember that it was far to the east that the wonderful breed lived, the breed from which those older mares believed Ilinga must have come.

46

Had this been the stallion from whom Winganna had stolen Ilinga's dam? He almost stopped to look round – and got a sharp bite for being so foolish. He was sure – quite sure – that this hulking grey was not Ilinga's sire. Suddenly he felt equally sure that he could give him a tremendous strike if he swung to one side quickly – for that heavy brute would not be able to stop . . .

Quickly swinging, pivoting, rearing, Wurring did get in a fierce – and lucky – strike above the iron-grey's eye. This only made the grey more insanely furious, but this time, feeling so elated at really hitting him, Wurring did manage to maintain his speed for a while, so a minute or so elapsed before he felt the flailing, striking hooves. He turned then, made a wild bite, got a hold and hung on as long as his strength allowed.

The iron-grey had no feelings of respect for a valiant young fighter. He soon taught Wurring that, if he wished to remain alive, he had better do what he was made to do, and not try to hit back.

Wurring had cut him above the eye and drawn blood on his neck. While these wounds hurt, the grey might easily get so savage that he killed.

They went on and on and Wurring began to get very tired. They crossed a great plain with a clump of trees in the centre of it. There was a chance to rest in these trees because the iron-grey stopped and looked around, as though searching for something.

Wurring stood, breathing deeply and keeping a careful watch on his evil-tempered captor. Was he dreaming, or was there a faint, lingering fragrance? A vision of Ilinga rose like a ghost in the air in front of him.

In a moment the grey was driving him on again, lashing out, biting.

Wurring went. As he left, he noticed that there were a lot more hoofmarks among those trees than they had made. Then, staring at him out of the damp earth, was one imprint of Ilinga's near fore foot.

They went on and on, all through that day. By evening

47

Wurring was very lame. His shoulder was on fire, and he was so tired that he got slower and slower. Fortunately the iron-grey had quietened down too.

They were going through wide-spaced snowgums now, and the sudden call of a mopoke made both horses shy. The mopoke must have started moving along with them, because it called continually. Once, when it was on a low branch, the iron-grey took a flying leap at it.

Wurring was surprised. Though the horses sometimes chased brolgas or emus for a game, he had never seen a brumby chase any other wild creature out of sheer bad temper. Wurring, young though he was, felt that a horse who could attack a bird did not seem to be part of his world. Every bird and beast, even the very storms could turn against him.

The owl flew out of reach, and his double call mocked the horse. The birds, Wurring knew, were wiser than horses. They were thought to be wiser than any animal, for, flying through the air, they saw so much of the world, could see what was happening everywhere, knew what was going to happen. Also they never forgot anything, and seemed to live forever.

The mopoke hooted again, and the horse screamed with rage. Wurring shivered. How could any horse defy those who might hold the secret of his life?

His ears pricked. Had there been a far-off neigh? He got a nip from behind to urge him on. They must be getting to their journey's end. He felt a sudden surge of interest. Could it be that he would learn, now, where Ilinga had come from?

As they dropped down into a valley, the moon rose – the moon rose over this country that must have made Ilinga. There was another neigh from below, but the iron-grey did not answer, and though the mopoke still mocked him, and he made another rush at it, he did not roar again. It was as if he wished to surprise his herd by arriving unexpectedly. Wurring did not think it would be a very pleasant surprise. He kicked stones down the slope on purpose, to warn them.

Even if this were where Ilinga had come from, he was sure that the iron-grey was not her father, so the mystery still existed. Either she had *not* come from his herd, or he had stolen her mother. It seemed to him to be very important to know, and to know why all the birds and the other horses seemed to think of Ilinga as coming from a great past, and going to fulfil some important future. Were any of the horses, down below, of the same blood as Ilinga?

The slope grew steeper. His near shoulder hurt so much that he could barely step on to that leg. The sweat of pain began to drip off him. The pain shot, burning from shoulder to knee, almost beyond bearing, but if he slowed up, he got another, harder bite.

Then they were on the valley floor, and the horse stopped for a moment. If he had hoped that his herd did not know that it was he who was coming, the mopoke spoilt his plan, for it sat high in a tree and every call it gave was a warning.

Wurring knew that his herd must fear him.

He was forced to walk on again, and the agony of his leg put all else out of his mind, till suddenly he saw the ring of watching eyes, the faces of well over a dozen mares and young colts and fillies.

*   *   *

While Wurring was so lame that he could barely move, he meant less than nothing to the iron-grey stallion – less than nothing, except as a bait that might attract Ilinga.

Wurring's shoulder was so bad that in fact it was difficult for him to graze. He had to stay close to the stream, or he would not have got a drink. He grew thin and weak, and his coat looked miserable. The nights were getting colder already, suggesting that winter was coming early. He was going to be in a very poor state to stand a hard winter.

Wurring did not think about this, himself, but he did know that he got weaker every day, and that, unless he was very strong, he would never escape nor ever possibly defeat the iron-grey.

The young ones of the herd came to him when the stallion was some distance off.

It was one of the fillies who led him – hopping on three legs – to where sweet grass grew very close to the water so that he could graze and drink too. Later two fillies grazed with him most of the time, but neither were like Ilinga.

The days went by. The iron-grey expecting Ilinga to come to find Wurring, and Wurring unable to do anything, hoping that the birds would tell her of the danger – and yet certain that danger would not stop her.

She might never find the way.

7: *To the East*

Ilinga went quietly, swiftly out of Ravine, wondering what had happened to cause such fear in the Ravine herd, and anxious to get far away before anything befell her. Her head was set for Numeramang, but it was unlikely that she would get there before daylight. In her mind she could see Wurring there, and it was not till she had crossed the Tumut River that she got any feeling that he might have been hurt, or that he might have gone looking for her. The cold touch of this water which she and Wurring had crossed together once, and in which the iron-grey had made her stand, suddenly sent cold fear into her mind. She hurried on even faster towards Numeramang, up through the timber, down into thick gullies, up again and down.

Once, just at dawn, a lyrebird hopped across her path, in a deep-cleft valley, its tail was not spread and it hung as though disjointed. Presently she heard its voice from somewhere in the deep bush, not mocking, but speaking of winter and darkness. She heard the sound fading into the distance as she trotted along, but the more distant the voice became, the more insistent was the message, and the more it seemed to be for her.... Winter ... and darkness ... the departing light of the sun. ... She shivered.

Even before she reached Numeramang, she knew she would not find any horses. The creeping skin on her own back, when she thought of the dead horse lying there, told her that none of Winganna's herd would stay.

She had to look into the empty plain from behind a candlebark, just look, to be sure that no one was there. The light was strong, and the big plain was clearly to be seen.

No living horse was there.

She almost swung round to hurry away, but where should she go? She stood wondering if there were any of Winganna's herd nearby at all, and then some instinct told her to look and see if there might be some of Wurring's tracks which she could follow.

She began to move out, looking for the tracks, but she stopped again. If she went out on to the plain, she, herself, would be visible to any eyes, just one lone filly in the empty plain where the dead Winganna lay.

Fear was beginning to eat into her, but she had no idea where Wurring had gone, and the only way to find out was by tracking him. Wurring had not been far from her when the iron-grey started to chase her. In fact she remembered hearing

52

the sound of his galloping hooves, just as she turned to run for her life.

Shaking all over, she walked out till she was quite close to the dead horse, right at the place where she had been standing when the iron-grey first stared at her.

Yes! There was a track of Wurring's. She followed the rather indistinct marks of several galloping strides, then there were blurred markings, and dragged-out lines of a scuffle, and the milling around of several horses. Yarran's hoofmarks were particularly clear.

Ilinga searched and searched, but she could not piece together any information out of all these hoofmarks. It seemed that Wurring and Yarran and several others might have spent some time near the creek. A number of horses had moved to and fro there, but it was almost impossible to pick out any individual tracks.

She felt intensely uncomfortable, as though unknown eyes were watching her, but she had to go on looking for some clear tracks of Wurring's to tell her where he had gone.

In fact there were no other horses near – none of Winganna's herd wanted to be close to where he had been killed – there was just the feeling of eyes, eyes, eyes watching, so that her skin prickled. Oh fear – what was fear? But fear was there, and real – fear in the whisper of the candlebark leaves, fear in the blocks of shadow cast by the trees around the moonlit plain. She almost turned and galloped away, senselessly.

At last she realized she was never going to find any clear tracks, and the terror of her aloneness was getting too great. She crept among the trees. There she stood, irresolute, for she had no idea where to go.

Perhaps she would make down into the forest country. At least she would be safe there. So she started to go along ridges they had travelled last winter. For the rest of that day she wandered through forests, and not one hoofmark did she find. By night time she felt that she could not bear to be alone any longer, but she simply did not know where any of her herd had gone.

53

She was trembling with fear of the night, so she hid herself in some thick black sallees. At first the silence oppressed her, then the night sounds seemed to become more noticeable, the quark of a possum, the hoot of a mopoke, the snuffling and grubbing sound of a wombat, the repeated quarks of the giant glider, and then the mournful howl of a dingo and an answering cry from far away. Ilinga knew all these wild creatures, and felt safer, happier, less alone. If she listened carefully she might hear some news of the wandering herd. She might get some idea of where she should search, or even of why Wurring had vanished?

The dingo howled to the moon of loss and sorrow.

The moon seemed to weave light through the thick, dark leaves. A beam of its light fell straight on to her – cold, a shaft of moonlight. She pawed restlessly, and saw her own foreleg silvered by the moon.

The moon, the moon, this was all that the night voices seemed to say, but, as the moon's shaft passed over her, she felt as though she had known something a long time ago and forgotten it, and that now she must remember, walk along old, old tracks, play out an old, old story.

Without knowing why, barely knowing that she was moving, she began to walk eastward, eastward through the night, eastward into memory, eastward into an old legend.

Dawn was breaking when she reached the Tumut River – and there she smelt the familiar comforting smell of Yarran. She searched around for tracks and found several hoofmarks of Yarran's, heading downstream, but there was absolutely no sign of Wurring's track with hers. She followed for quite a distance, but the rising sun seemed to call her 'east, east', and at last, when she had gone about a mile, she was quite certain that she was not going to find any sign of Wurring and not going to catch up with Yarran, she answered the call of the sun and turned back. Then she struck east again, towards Ravine.

As she reached the top of the ridge, the sun shone dazzlingly in her eyes, blindingly, so that she kept seeing a chestnut horse galloping towards her, with the sun burning in his mane. Golden horse – but he was not there.

She went along the ridge above Ravine rather slowly, wondering whether she should go down into the valley or cut around the top of it. But perhaps the horses that lived there might have seen something ... heard something. ... What was it that had so frightened them?

Standing there, thinking, she remembered that older grey mare who had called so loudly of loss and sorrow, that first time they had visited Ravine. If she could find that mare, or even another young filly ... She began to go down very slowly.

There was silence below her. Even for a moment the dawn birds were not singing. The solitude seemed to be endless.

The cliffs opposite were dark, not yet touched by the sun. She looked at them often, as she went quietly downwards. She was sure a horse was standing on top of one. Also she became sure that someone was near her, someone had moved. Then, as she stepped into an almost open patch, a neigh rang out from the opposite cliff. She stopped, as though made of that dark rock herself. The neigh was warning other horses that she was coming. Had the Ravine herd posted sentries like those of the flocks of white cockatoos?

Fear! Her hide felt as though ants were crawling all over it. She would roll when she was on flatter ground, but one cannot roll fear away even if the hide stops crawling. Her sweat began to run in spite of the fact that the morning was fresh and cold. There was a movement on the cliffs opposite. Yes: a light-coloured horse was walking across the top of them. It must have been watching very carefully, because her dark brown coat would not show up much in timber. She shivered as though the sun had gone under a cloud for a moment, but she kept on walking down.

The herd were on the top grassy flat where Wurring and she had galloped and played. Ilinga watched them from the trees, but they had heard the warning neigh, and were all uneasy. Then another young colt joined the group, from the forest quite close to her, and she knew that the whole herd would soon know that she was standing there.

She walked out into the open.

The herd stood stock still and looked at her, then the stallion began to come towards her. He was a big strong bay, strong, very strong. What he if would not let her go on her way to find Wurring? Her only safety lay in play.

She cantered gaily towards the herd, keeping going even when the old grey mare threw up her head and neighed a queer call, the call that was a lament for the dangers that the last of the breed of the Moon would have to try to survive, if ever that which was said to be going to happen would come true. This high, crying neigh filled Ilinga with dread, though she really did not know what it was all about.

She had been seen now, by them all, so she must play the gay filly, have no cares, let no one see that for her the sun was not shining. She must canter with rhythm and joy. After all she had been gay and happy only a few days ago. She would dance, and rear, and gallop... and perhaps she would learn what had made this herd so nervous, perhaps hear news of Wurring.

Then, as she got nearer, she nearly stopped in mid-rear, nearly dropped to her feet and stared.

There, with this herd, were three fillies from Winganna's herd – the three who had been most jealous of her friendship with Wurring, and one of them had been a foal whose mother had arrived at Numeramang on the same night as Ilinga and her dam.

Even though they had bitten and kicked at her all this summer, Ilinga was overjoyed to see them. However, perhaps she should not let the stallion know that they had belonged to the same herd, and as she pivotted, and leapt, and reared – with that stallion following her – she suddenly thought how jealous they had been of her. She must be careful.

When she joined them, they did not snap at her. She tried to lead them all off in play and dance, but, until the stallion started to leap and pivot, they seemed to be too nervous for such games. Even when he played, the mares and young ones took a while to be anything but half-hearted, and they kept looking up at the cliffs, as though they were afraid of something or someone coming from up above.

All that day Ilinga learnt nothing except that every mare and young one was afraid. At night the three fillies from her own herd let her stand with them for warmth, but she was no nearer to finding Wurring. Before sunrise, in heavy darkness, she moved silently away, climbed up the eastern side of the valley. Once up on top she would go steadily towards the lightening sky – east, east, east.

No one seemed to notice her going, which was good, because the heavy bay stallion would certainly not have let her leave, had he been awake.

She was half way up the long climb when a neigh rang out from below, and the sound rolled all around the cliffs. The grey mare had woken and she called and called – called a warning of a stallion. Ilinga stopped. Was this what had frightened the herd – a fierce stallion? She listened to every sound and its echo. As she stood listening, the old legend seemed to wrap itself around her. The vanishing sun...a young horse...a fierce stallion...the sun...the moon...a strange night...a strange light ... but she must not stand still because soon they would discover that she had gone, and the stallion would come after her.

Then a mopoke called above her head. Ilinga dared not wait another moment.

She climbed as quickly as she could, and as silently.

The mopoke did not follow for long. He would know that he could give her whereabouts away, but the mopoke knew that the iron-grey had lost Ilinga and taken Wurring. He knew, too, in his wisdom, that if Ilinga went searching she might be recaptured by that fierce iron-grey. So the mopoke's calls only gave Ilinga a feeling of danger, a feeling that she was going in the right direction for Wurring, but that she was being warned against going. And all the time she had the sensation of having done all this before – or perhaps of having to do it because it all had to happen.

Then she was in sunlight again, blinded by the oblique sun-

57

shafts. She trotted on, with the sun in her eyes, in the direction which she knew she must go . . . only because she knew it.

There was a small plain encircled by silver snowgums. It was so familiar to her that she stopped there, trying to remember, trying to remember where she had come from. She had been sure that the iron-grey was going to take her back there. Had he taken Wurring there instead of her? And, if so, *where*?

East? All her instincts told her to go east.

The further she went, the stronger became the feeling that she knew this land, that she had been this way before. There were tracks, and her hooves seemed to know them. It was as though a voice called her, but it was only the sun, and, as the sun climbed higher overhead and sank in the west, she still kept going eastward. On she went, till night fell, and she slept among some thick snowgums.

The rising sun called her, and she started on again. She stopped once to drink at a still pool and saw, mirrored there, a filly that was no longer a gangling, leggy yearling. Just as Wurring had thought his father was looking at him from the Tumut River, she thought an older filly was near her. She could not know that in these last few days, when she had seen Winganna killed, been captured herself, by the iron-grey, and escaped from him, and then searched alone for Wurring, she had grown up. She could not know that the strange quality which some of the horses had seen in her, even when she was a foal, was now becoming more apparent – the irradiant glow of her coat, the deeply lit eyes, the rhythm of movement.

Twice, that morning, she heard a stallion neigh, somewhere quite close.

8: *Young Brown Stallion*

A strange stallion, never showing himself, followed Ilinga for miles. She could hear him: sometimes she could smell him. He made no effort to go quietly. Often he called her, a soft attractive call, but she could never see him.

He must have seen her, or else how would he be following her? ... Why?

How? Why? The snowgums moving in a cool wind did not answer these questions. The sparrow hawk hovering above for most of the day told nothing, but its far-seeing eyes were watching all the time.

Would she stand still, and wait to see what that horse would do – what he looked like?

She stopped in a small glade where a clear stream ran. . . . She waited, she drank, she waited.

The horse called softly. Once she thought she saw his eyes, perhaps the dark brown of his forehead. It was silly of her to have stopped in a glade, even in so small a glade. She could be seen, and the watcher remain invisible. She pressed herself backwards into the trees and waited again, peering out through the thick leaves. Perhaps the horse might show himself?

She waited and waited. The trees all around her were very thick, so she would hear him if he came round behind or to either side. Complete silence closed in. The sparrow hawk hovered, but no bird made any sound and no animal stirred.

Ilinga was tired, and her eyes closed occasionally. She opened them – and there, standing as though unaware of his strength and his own youth and beauty, and yet supremely happy because of all these things, was a brown horse, almost as dark as herself. Half-shy, half-confident, he reared before her. His strong muscles rippled, his mane and tail shone.

Ilinga looked, and her eyes opened wider and wider, but she kept perfectly still. Here was a most beautiful young horse, inviting her to go with him. Would he allow her to escape and continue her search for Wurring?

She remained quite still.

The handsome young brown looked disappointed. Then, after a few soft neighs, he walked towards the thick leaves and branches where she was hidden.

She pressed backwards, managed to turn and force her way through the next clump into less thick timber. Then she turned east again, and kept going.

The young horse followed.

What would happen when they came to open country? But how did she know so certainly that they must come to great, rolling snowgrass hills and plains? Her one anxiety was how she would get away from that brown horse.

His eyes were kind ... perhaps he would not try to hold her ... but Ilinga felt sure he wanted her for his herd.

Presently there was another soft neigh, asking her to go with him. She began to canter, wherever the ground allowed it. The horse cantered too.

The glades in the valleys were becoming more open, the valley floors were wider. The whole character of the country was changing. They would soon be out on those high, wide plains.

The valleys became wider and wider: the trees got less. Now Ilinga was cantering in the open.

A horse when alone feels the touch of the wind so much. The wind's touch may be a challenge, offering a race, it may be life and the whole tempestuous fury and glory of life for a stallion and his mares, or for young animals just leaving the herd, but for one alone, the wind's touch is the touch of fear.

Ilinga had been very afraid, but while she kept moving the fear had not eaten into her like it did at Numeramang. Now there was this fear seeming to enfold her, coming on the air of the wide spaces, the air that moved over rolling grey-green hills, moved up open, treeless valleys where the water glinted cold ... fear on the cold wind.

Just then, from behind and not very far off, came another stallion's neigh.

Ilinga heard the hoofbeat behind her check and stop, as the brown listened. She guessed that he would stand for a moment, looking around, and she would have time to hide in the last of the trees.

That second stallion called again. She was almost certain that it was the horse from Ravine.

The brown stallion looked round for her and, being unable to see her, seemed to forget everything but the necessity of finding her. He searched around for her tracks and began to follow them. Just then the big bay came into sight.

Ilinga watched the brown. He heard the other horse: he swung round. She felt a flutter of hope that the nice-looking brown would win, and she crept away, while neither of them were looking, and trotted on.

Presently she heard the sound of fighting behind her, but all her hair was standing on end already, and with the aloneness of the high, wild country, for she had passed through the last of the trees and now there was nowhere to hide at all.

If it had not been that she longed so deeply to find Wurring, she could never have forced herself over the open plains where the wind cried of winter and sorrow, and she was just one filly, utterly alone, seeking the horse who had been the sun, and life itself, to her, ever since she had been a foal.

She still had no clear picture of where she was going, just that certainty that she was trotting towards the country from which she had come, and that she must find this country if she were to find Wurring. The thought of Wurring, standing against the sun, his mane and forelock on fire with light, seemed to call her on and on, on and on over that cold, open country.

Then, beyond the sound of her own hoofbeats, it seemed to her that she heard another beat. Her heart lurched within her chest. She cast a wild look over her shoulder. The bay from Ravine was following some way behind, galloping fast, and, behind him, was the brown.

She began to race desperately.

Unending miles of open country seemed to stretch ahead of her, but to the north there might be cover. She swung that way and the horses followed.

Ilinga was surprised to find that the bay was not gaining on her, and the realization came to her that she, herself, might be very fast. Another glance behind told her that the brown was catching up to the bay. They would fight again, and while they were fighting she would be able to get her breath, perhaps get right away.

She heard a furious scream. The bay was refusing to stop to fight properly. The brown was trying to force him. Then suddenly the brown darted ahead of the bay and after Ilinga.

This time Ilinga did not hurry. It might be better if they both almost caught up with her. The bay would have to stop and fight... She *had* to find Wurring... Wurring with the sunlight in his free-flowing mane... Wurring.

Both horses were getting closer. The brown was coming up on one side of her, the bay on the other. Perhaps they were not going to stop and fight. She felt desperate and angry. She dug in her toes and, with a few proppy strides, managed to stop. The stallions almost crashed into each other. Surely they might fight now, and she get away. But they only watched her.

She began to move on, and they moved on with her – north instead of east – and Ilinga saw no way of escaping.

* * *

There was no way of escape for days, neither northwards, in the trees, nor eastward in the vast spaces. At last it became clear to Ilinga that, whether these horses came with her or not, she must seek Wurring.

Every sign seemed to tell of an early winter, every bird cried of cold and snow, and one flight of mountain duck went overhead with their loud honks sounding an ominous warning. Their cries seemed to be of the vanishing sun. Ilinga listened, and saw their patterned flight in the sky. Could something dreadful be going to happen to Wurring, for Wurring was the sun?

The sky looked laden with snow, and the wind howled round rocks, round the shoulders of mountains, down narrow valleys.

The two stallions were getting nervous. For Ilinga even fear seemed to have gone: there was just a burning purpose. She trotted on across the path of the wind, mane and tail tossed, recognizing all the country she crossed, as though in a sort of dream, yet never coming to the end of the dream – never finding the place she had come from and where she believed Wurring to be.

Where had she come from? What did the place look like? The wind cried an eerie: 'Wh-e-r-e, oh wh-e-r-e.'

They had gone for many miles without seeing a sign of other horses. Just at the moment in which Ilinga saw the first track, she also noticed the hollow thud that her hooves made on the ground. Was there something she remembered? Hollow-sounding ground?

Suddenly she felt completely certain that she was near Wurring and she began to gallop. The country had become steeper. There were trees, scrub: a cliff of streaked and broken rock reared out of tree heads that were tossing in the wind. Thick wattles whipped her shoulders and flanks as she galloped up on to a ridge. The stallions were behind. She knew, by now, that she could race that bay – though perhaps not out-last him.

The wind cried around that cliff, and then the big, white flakes of snow began to fall.

Wurring must be found before the snow covered all the world, before it became impossible for a horse to travel over the hills. Ilinga felt the cold flakes on her back, and sped faster up the hill.

She was quite close under the cliff – it seemed to rise straight across the valley that must lie between this ridge and the next one. She reached the ridge top, and the ground fell away in front of her, steeply down. She stiffened her forelegs, trying to slow or even stop. The ground was damp. A thick rope of wild raspberry tripped her. She made a quick jump, and, as she landed, her feet began to slide. There seemed to be a long, long slope of grass and bark streamers that had fallen off the tall trees.

She was sliding fast. She missed crashing into a ribbongum by flinging herself sideways. Then she was off balance, going faster and faster, sliding on one flank, and the slope was getting steeper and steeper.

Then there was no longer the ground beneath her: she was

64

falling through the air. She saw the cliff above her, and the snow-laden sky. Then all at once the dark day became darker. She was falling down in a narrow place. The light of that snowy sky was far above.

9: *Vanishing Stream*

The two stallions reached the top of the ridge only a few moments after Ilinga did, but she had already vanished from sight. The brown horse was going faster than the bay, and he slithered at the top of the ridge too, but Ilinga had broken that rope of wild raspberry, so that was not there to trip him, and he did not begin to slide out of control.

Both horses started down, but they went slowly and they were puzzled. There was the mark of Ilinga's slide on the grass and in among the bark streamers, but it was not possible to understand how she was no longer to be seen.

Down they went, slowly, carefully, the bay keeping his distance behind, for there was no reason to look for a fight when the filly, over whom they might have fought, was no longer there. At the beginning he had felt quite confident that his greater weight would make it almost unnecessary to do more than strike a few blows, and the young brown stallion would know that he was unable to have that filly, but while they had followed her he had learnt that the filly and the brown stallion were both faster than he, and the filly had some quality which might make her most difficult to win. Something which the Ravine horse did not acknowledge, but which was really quite apparent, was that the brown stallion had a superiority of intelligence which had put him into position of leader, just as much as his speed had.

As soon as they realized that Ilinga had really vanished, those two horses heard the moan of the wind again, felt the cold flutter of the snow at their faces, the solid cold of it gripping their backs. Flutter of fear, grip of terror; the winter was coming: the filly had gone.

Fear ... terror began to shake the bay from Ravine. The

brown horse's mind was filled with the necessity of finding
Ilinga. For him, Ilinga was mystery and beauty, and perhaps
had the added attraction of being unobtainable because she
must belong so profoundly to someone else.

The descent into the valley became very steep and now the

snow began to lie on the ground. The two horses found themselves sliding. The brown checked himself and set off across the hillside at an angle. A wombat's track helped him.

The bay was a much more clumsy mover – also heavier. His feet broke the edge of the track away and suddenly he was sliding fast. The brown watched with great interest ... Ilinga had slipped ... Ilinga had disappeared, but they had already moved over to a less steep slope than the one she went down. Whatever had happened to her, might not happen to the bay.

The bay simply stuck in a bush. What snow had coated the bush now fell on to him. His efforts to get up churned up the earth.

At last he was up and shaking himself. The snow fell more thickly: the filly was nowhere to be seen: Ravine lay a long way behind him, Ravine and his mares. He had had enough.

He took one last look down into the empty valley, shook the snow out of his forelock, and turned for home.

The brown stallion watched him go, but only for a moment, then he went on down into that knife-cut valley.

There was no valley floor, only a creek. He had to climb up a few feet again, to get a slope on to which he could cling with his hooves, and work his way downstream, to a point below where Ilinga had slid. There, even if he could not find her, he must see her tracks.

The wind could not touch him down there, though its sound was hollow up above him. The big snowflakes dropped straight down between the tall trees, melted as they touched the dark stream, lay on leaves and ground, log and branch.

The snow on his hide, and the hollow roar of the wind, made the brown horse so nervous that he was ready to leap in the air even if an unusually large snowflake fell on his back. Though he listened very carefully, there was no other sound except the wind's. He neighed once, and stopped so that he would be sure to hear even the faintest sound. There was no answer, and certainly no noise that Ilinga might have made, had she been climbing up out of the valley.

He went on, past ribbongums that reached up out of the

deep valley, up, up, towards the grey sky that was half-vanished in the dense-falling flakes. Wild raspberries and bark streamers tied themselves around his legs, fallen branches tripped him.

The great cliff was towering above, its rocks like no rocks he had ever seen before. It closed the end of the valley. He must be right where Ilinga had fallen, and yet there was no sign of her, nothing at all. She was not lying there, hurt. There was not one track to tell that she had been there. He searched on one side of the creek, then jumped over on to the other side and searched that. Soon the snow would cover even his own tracks . . . cover everything until the spring came.

This cliff ended the valley. The brown horse took a few more uncertain steps. He was walking down beside a creek and yet a cliff was right across the valley . . . The filly had simply disappeared. The air was so full of snow that the falling flakes made him feel dizzy, lost. Everything was uncertain.

He looked up the slope where Ilinga had surely fallen. Snow went into his eyes, this straight falling snow that made his head reel. He took a few more steps forward, and then something told him to stop. One forefoot was still stepping out, but he stopped it in mid-air.

Underneath that hoof there was only space.

He looked down. His head spun and he stepped backwards. There was a great hole right in front of him.

It was impossible to swing round, in this steep-sided cleft, and thus get away forever. He backed, but then he had to see into that hole again. Placing his hooves with great care, he walked forward, inch by inch, till he could see in again. The waters of the creek went hurtling, splashing into the hole, water splashing on to white rocks, and then vanishing into darkness. Snowflakes fell straight down into that hole too.

Water falling, snow falling, everything disappearing. The brown horse backed away again, shaking. He started to climb back up the slope. After he had scrambled up a few feet, he stopped . . . and stood . . . young, handsome, intelligent horse, so wet from the falling snow that his coat looked almost black, except for white flecks, and now the snow was matting his mane and forelock. He stood...

The filly he had been following for days had fallen down this slope.... She was following someone else, as though her life depended on it... but she was beautiful. She had gone and he must find her.

There was absolute silence, lonely and fearful silence. The bay had gone, and he was alone, and then there came a long drawn-out, eerie cry of the wind around the cliff.

The brown horse felt the sweat of fear stinging and burning against the cold touch of the snow, but he turned down again towards the hole where the creek vanished beneath the cliff. The ground was becoming more and more slippery with the snow. He pressed each hoof into the wet earth, as he walked, clinging on to the steep slope, and he went to the edge.

There was no other hoofmark except his, not any track of Ilinga even right at the edge. The only unusual marks that he could see were lower. A wide shelf of earth looked as if something had slid right over its surface, and there was a lump of mud slowly being washed off one of the shining white rocks. Perhaps there was a scratch mark on another.

If Ilinga had fallen, where had she gone? It would have been difficult for her to climb out. Also there would have been plenty of marks if she had scrambled out of that hole. He stood staring at the dark cavern into which the creek vanished, and the thick snowflakes were falling, falling, everything was moving. The cliff, the cavern, the tall ribbongums, and the steep hillsides were whirling around him.

Suddenly he called, wild and loud. The echo came rolling back at him out of the cave, then rang off the cliff, rolled round the valley.

The filly was not his. To follow her was like trying to catch and hold a moonbeam. For her there was some other tremendous attraction that drew her and drew her... the rising sun in the east... something... someone. She was not his, perhaps never would be, yet he could not drag himself away.

He stepped right back from the hole, jumped the creek, and

stood waiting and watching, waiting while the snow fell softly, steadily, and without sound.

He watched and waited for hours and nothing happened at all, no one came: nothing could be heard but the wind. At last he climbed some distance up the opposite side of the valley from which they had come down. He found a place where the ground flattened out a little. Here there was some grass, if he nosed around in the snow, and he could still see that hole at the foot of the cliff.

It was as though he expected Ilinga to form like a ghost, in the darkness of the cave, and emerge as solid flesh. This was a dream, but he could not leave.

Aloneness pressed in on him, and the winter snow clouds closed down and down. The ground became white and the only marks were where the drips fell from the trees and melted the snow through to the earth. Silence, silence and gradually night closed in while still the snow fell.

All night that young stallion stood beneath the trees, slowly becoming shrouded in snow. In the morning there was no other horse to disturb the white stillness.

Not a very great deal of snow had fallen and, though the sky was heavy laden, no flakes fell as daylight came. The young horse climbed higher on to really flat ground, and scratched around for more grass.

It was not possible for him to leave that cave where the river vanished . . . where the filly had vanished too. Something called him back. As the second night fell, he had gone to the shelter of the same ribbongum, and was waiting. Snow was falling again, but the wind had ceased to cry. The whisper of snow sliding off leaves was the only sound. Winter had come. Winter's snow would bind the land. Only the birds would move over the great white hills. A horse would be caught and held – held till he died. Every nerve, from the tips of his hooves to his ears, to his withers, his back, told him to go, to make for low country quickly while he could still move through the snow, but he waited through the long, dark night.

10: *A Dream or a Memory*

The dark day became darker. Snowflakes still spattered her, then Ilinga felt a crushing bump. The bump was on sloping earth, otherwise bones might have been broken, as it was, she slid.

Rocks caught at her, spinning her, but they broke the speed of her slide. Finally she crashed on to cold wet rocks. Water sprayed over her, and the only light was a small patch above and to one side. A dark rock roof sheltered her from the falling snow.

She felt around with her hooves for solid footholds. It was all rock – uneven, with spaces between, and very slippery. She leapt up, shaking all over. She began to slip and slide her way towards the patch of light, hooves scrabbling on rocks. When one foreleg slipped between two boulders, and twisted, she knew she must be more careful. Careful ... but there was a glassy surface of water on the white rocks from which she must jump to get on to that sloping patch of earth on which she had landed and then slipped.

She stood measuring up the distance, and as she stood, the picture of the place where she had fallen, the cliff, the vanishing stream, the cave in which she stood, all seemed to sort itself out in her mind as a dream or a memory of something she had seen before ... some dark hollow she had walked into with her mother?

Her eyes were becoming used to the darkness. She looked into the cavern and felt quite sure that she had been in something like this before. Then she turned to climb out ... but what was below? Where did that cavern lead? Where had she come from? Where was Wurring?

Slowly she turned and began to move with great care over the slippery rocks. Now there was just nothing in her mind except that she had seen whatever she was coming to before, and that she must find Wurring at the end of the darkness.

After she had gone some yards, the floor of the cave became smoother, still slippery, but smooth, and there was a smell of wombat. All the fears with which she had lived for these past days, were pushed away by certainty. She was coming to the end of her journey. It was as though she were drawn along by some magnetism that made her forget fear, and darkness, and being enclosed – as though she were doing something that she had always known she would do but had not been able to remember. This certainty that she would find Wurring after she had gone through the darkness was all part of the stories which the wind and the grass had sung, which had been in the lyrebird's dance, and the moon dance of the brolgas.

Something stronger than a dream had possession of Ilinga. As though she had already seen him, she knew that Wurring was ahead, in a wide sunny valley – a valley in which at least her feet would know the way.

She simply knew, just as she knew that she was alive, that Wurring was ahead.

There must have been some narrow cracks above her head, through which light could filter, because there were only small areas of absolute darkness, and Ilinga's eyes had become attuned to it.

The floor of the cave grew very rough again, where rocks must have fallen. The creek rushed and foamed beside her as she scrambled and slid over the boulders. This rough part stretched interminably. As it went on and on she began to feel almost afraid again – afraid that she could not get through, afraid that she would not get back over the rocks down which she was sliding – then the certainty of Wurring being ahead flooded through her, and she strove on and on.

At last she was on smooth ground again – and there was a faint light ahead.

It was only then that she began to feel the presence of the encompassing dark, feel it like a thick curtain behind her. She started to hurry – and heard her hooves echoing over the quietening sound of the stream. The sound made her be more careful. Others would be ahead as well as Wurring.

The light ahead grew more definite, a patch getting bigger and bigger. There was a bend in the tunnel, and once she was round it, she could see a widening cavern ahead.

Memory came in a flash that caused her to stop and then go far more slowly, for she could see in her mind an open cavern and her mother standing in it. In her mind's picture there was a sandy floor, a nice rolling place, and it was all sheltered from

74

rain and snow. Could she be coming to this cavern from its back?

As she drew closer, she could see the silhouette of a horse against the light – a horse sheltering in the cave. Her feet moved slower and slower, more and more carefully. The shape against the light was that of the iron-grey stallion.

Ilinga stopped, a surge of fear forcing her to gasp for breath. She tried to become still, afraid that her very fear was strong enough to be smelt, or heard, or felt, down by the cave opening. She pressed herself against the rock wall, and the cold of it bit into her hide, but the hard rock steadied her. She would just have to wait till the stallion moved away.

The iron-grey was restless. Over and over again she thought he would go, but he only walked a few steps and threw his head up. At last Ilinga realised that he was worrying about the snow, and that he probably would not move while the snow fell – unless he decided that the time had come to take his herd to lower country.

Ilinga waited. The stream moved past her, hour after hour; the day faded away, and the snowflakes still fell outside the cave. She knew that the only time when she could seek Wurring would be at night, when the iron-grey would probably be sleeping – and now it looked as though he might not move. Darkness fell and it was still snowing.

She was beginning to feel desperate when at last she saw the iron-grey walk off. Apparently he did not like snow, he shook himself all the time.

When he did not come back she ventured further along the tunnel, then slowly into the cavern and right to the opening and stood pressed against some dark rock. She looked out over the valley and once more memory sprang alive with pictures, some clear and some much hazier. Undoubtedly she had been here before, but she felt angrily certain that the iron-grey was not her sire.

Her eyes were searching for Wurring – expecting a gleaming horse, even though no horse could gleam in twilight and a snowfall. Then she saw him, and it was as though he knew she

75

had come, because he was standing with his head thrown up, and his ears pricked. He looked so vital, just for that moment, that she did not realize how gaunt he was, nor did she notice, all at once, that he was standing on three legs. She saw all this when he hopped himself around to look in her direction, and the horrifying realization came to her that a horse on three legs could not get over the long stretch of slippery boulders, over one enormous rock that had blocked the tunnel, or up out of the mouth of it.

She would have to wait till dark to go over to Wurring, unless he felt her presence and hopped towards her. She waited, keeping a careful eye out for the iron-grey.

Then she saw that iron-grey walking back towards the cave again. The only thing she could do was to back quickly into the tunnel. She dared not turn. She must watch to see if he noticed her movement. He came walking along without any change of expression, without any sign of interest, a bored, bad-tempered-looking horse. He came on his own, no mare apparently wanted to be with him. Ilinga had a last look at Wurring. Even thin, and gaunt, and very lame, and his lovely mane all matted with snow instead of gleaming and aflame, Wurring still had the power of life. She backed right into her tunnel and could no longer see his upflung head nor the restless lines of his hurt body.

She would have to hide herself, just where she had been before, where she could see the iron-grey and hope he would not smell or hear her. Once Ilinga nearly gave herself away, quite soon after the iron-grey came back, when the bats who must have lived in the roof of the cave decided that, even if the snow were falling, they would go out. As the first soft sound of wings whispered through the cave, she nearly moved, but then a high squeak and the musty smell told her what was above. They streamed past her head but she stood quiet. Perhaps she would learn something from them when they came back. Some of them flew so close to her that she could tell they knew she was there. Bats lived in a different world, not even the wide, high world of birds, but with their great sensitivity, they would learn many secrets.

Luckily for Ilinga there was water to drink. It was quite a long time since she had had time to graze. She began to realize that she was very hungry, as the hours of the night dragged by – hungry and tired. The iron-grey was asleep, she could tell that from the shape of his body, even though its outlines melted into the dark night and falling snows that showed at the cave opening. She dozed, herself, and every time she opened her eyes she found that stallion's shadowy shape in exactly the same position, against the patch of night sky.

The night passed slowly. She found herself wishing the bats would come back. Surely they would not flit about out there on the snow. Surely snowflakes would harm their frail wings.

Owl and bat light. They had left the cave just before dark: they would probably return at the first faint light. How much would they know? Would they flit around Wurring and convey to him the urgency of being careful, the urgency of not looking restless, of not letting the iron-grey know that she might be near.

No whisper of wings, no draught of moving air disturbed her through the night. It was just when there was a change in the patch of sky at the cave mouth that she heard them, the high squeaking, and then the wings. They circled her once – not for long enough to make the iron-grey suspect anything – and gentle wings wafted the air around her so that it was as if the little bats of the night air had given her the blessed feeling of confidence in her own self, made her feel her own entity, there in the eroding silence, and also her own belonging to her whole world. She heard the iron-grey snap angrily at the last bat of the flight, and was surprised. If he behaved like that, the help and support of·all the other wild creatures would not be for him. For her and for Wurring there would always be help from the birds and the animals.

The bats were gone, and she must move a little further into the tunnel before the light grew stronger.

There might be a niche in the wall, not too far back, from which she could still see the iron-grey . . . she had to turn and

77

walk away, because it was too dangerous to go backwards. Perhaps she would sidle and keep watching the iron-grey. She would see, then, if he noticed anything, if he appeared to be listening to sounds back in the cave.

She walked so slowly, putting down each hoof on the hard, slippery rock with such care that she was sure there was no sound, and the horse in the cave did not seem to notice anything.

She heard the soft movement of bats behind her and their squeaking. They had not settled down, yet, for their day of sleep. What did they know, these bats; they whose world was dark, and who flew with such delight in the twilit sky?

The bats felt her presence there, further up the cave and came flitting round her, never touching her, but their wings fanning the air all round, gently. And some of the secrets which the bats knew were alive in the cave that night, were whispered by their wingbeats. Into Ilinga's mind there rose a picture of the valley out beyond the cavern, the valley into which she had looked last night, but in her mind it was as she knew she had seen it in sunshine, and her dam was there with a noble, old stallion standing beside her, a tall brown horse who looked fast, really fast. Though she tried, she could not remember any more.

There was a sudden noise from the cave mouth. Ilinga had been thinking so hard about the sunny valley, trying so hard to remember, that she had not been watching the iron-grey, and now he was getting up from a roll, then moving as though to come further in.

All at once there was a cloud of bats all round his head. Ilinga saw him turn tail and go, go right out of the cave, and she saw the bats wheel against the lightening sky, and come back. Gently their wings fanned all around her, and then they were going up into their sleeping places in the roof.

The iron-grey did not return. Ilinga kept watching the cave mouth. She could see that the snow had stopped falling, but she knew she dared not go out till dark, even though the grey stallion did not come back.

As the hours passed the feeling that Wurring was so close, that this was the place from which she had come and that her search was over, grew so strong that she could not stop herself edging further and further down the tunnel. There was Wurring grazing by the creek...she was hungry too...She saw him lift his head and cautiously look towards the cave. There were two young fillies not far away from him. Ilinga barely noticed them: she was thinking of something else.

The stream flowed at her feet, smooth, dark and silent. Out beyond the cave it had a steely gleam where it caught what light there was in the grey sky. It joined the large creek just near where Wurring grazed. Ilinga dipped a forefoot into the dark water, put her nose down to touch it. The water at the junction of the Yarrangobilly and Tumut Rivers had sung to them once when she had plunged into it, following Wurring, the day they had galloped down from Ravine. Sometimes water held a picture of a horse. Ilinga had seen this as she drank at the Tumut – the older filly who looked over her shoulder.

She walked into the water now. The creek was deep and cold. It tugged at her legs. Surely the water should tell Wurring to come this way...that she was waiting. Then she saw him move, barely putting his near foreleg on the ground. She got out of the water and took a few more steps towards the wide, sandy mouth of the cave.

The bats must have been listening because several of them came flitting round her head, turning her back into safety.

She stood then, watching Wurring. There was no sunshine coming through that leaden sky, only the strange light that foretells snow, nothing really to flash in the lights of his hair. She had seen Wurring outlined by flames from the sun, but it was only in her eyes and memory that he burned with the sun's fire now.

He moved towards the river, limping, sometimes hopping on three legs. When he reached the water, he dropped his head to drink. Ilinga saw him become quite still just before his nose touched the water. Then up went his head as though he were

79

going to neigh, but no sound came, and he looked in her direction. She moved, hoping he might see the movement, and that no one else would. He stared, stared. Then he looked cautiously all around, and once more back towards her. He gave a little hop in her direction, but stopped and dropped his head to the water again.

Water that had passed by Ilinga was passing him. He held his head down to the stream for some time and then raised it to look searchingly towards the cave again, and his whole bearing was more alive. Then he drank deeply.

Ilinga knew, then, that he would stay quietly and wait, as she was waiting, for darkness. It was at that moment that she took more notice of the other two fillies. It was clear that they had seen that Wurring was excited by something.

The day wore on and on. Twilight came and the bats flew out of the cave, flew off in a little cloud. At last darkness fell, and the slow drift of flakes started again. On the other side of the cliff, the young brown stallion was starting his second night's long waiting, and Ilinga came out like a shadow, hooves soundless on the sand, and walked towards Wurring through the drifting flakes.

11: *Owl and Bat Light*

The iron-grey had left precipitately when the bats chased him.
He hated bats and was maddened to find that those who lived
in his favourite cave had got annoyed with him. There were
other caves opening off his valley, but none had such a sandy
floor on which to roll, and this sand was dry except when the

creek flooded after a sudden fall of heavy rain, or with melting snow. The iron-grey had not owned the valley for long enough to know about the floods, and the droughts, and the winds of this area, and he had made himself so hated by all the smaller animals and the birds that lived there, that they kept away from him so he did not learn from them what the weather was going to do.

He had spent the night in another cave, a very wide one with a little trickling stream in it. There was indeed more sand here than he remembered seeing before. He walked a little way up and found that it did not smell of bats; decided that it could be a better cave, except that he could not see so much of his valley. Anyway he had spent the night there, and all day he grazed about further and further from Ilinga's cave, sometimes climbing the hillsides where the snow did not lie so thickly.

That the clouds were ominous, promising danger from heavy snow, was a fact that even he could not fail to notice. It might soon be time to wonder if he should make down the valley. Last winter – his first winter after he had won the valley from that brown stallion – he had not had to go very far down the valley to find enough grass on which to live.

About mid-afternoon he walked upstream, wandering around the small groups of mares and foals. He did not go as far as Wurring, thus not entering into Ilinga's line of vision. There were those two fillies near Wurring. They were watching the young horse and he did seem to be restless.

The iron-grey watched the three of them. He had stolen Wurring to act as bait for the filly who had escaped him. Why was Wurring continually staring towards the cave?

The cave held bats. The iron-grey gave a disgusted shiver. Once again he saw Wurring throw his head up and look towards the sandy cave. The iron-grey walked a little closer to him. He was still out of Ilinga's line of sight.

The two fillies that were near Wurring were two of the neatest fillies in the herd, but they were nothing like that filly whom he had lost. *She* must have been the foal belonging to the strange and beautiful mare who had followed Winganna.

82

For that foolishness Winganna had died . . .

The mare, who had seemed to burn with the glow of a moonlight night, had been a most unusual mare, and the iron-grey knew that she had hated him. When he defeated the old stallion and took his herd and this valley, she had tried to escape . . . galloping away . . . but she could not escape *him*. Her foal had been born soon after her mad gallop.

She had, of course, escaped when Winganna came, but then she must have died.

Already almost two years had passed. The iron-grey who had defeated the old brown stallion, owner of the valley, and from whom Winganna had been able to take that mare, had now killed Winganna, but . . . 'time passes, time passes' cried the currawongs in the sky above him. He too, would grow old. Perhaps he was already slower and heavier. Perhaps he had never possessed all that was necessary to be king of his surroundings – certainly he had never had the leaping flame of life that had burned in Wurring.

The iron-grey looked at Wurring and gave himself an angry shake. Even though that chestnut colt looked as if he would die before the winter was finished, there were those two fillies, the best of the herd, almost always near him. Obviously even when he was nearly dead he was an attractive horse. Why was he restless? Was it just that he was afraid of winter coming? The iron-grey nosed around for grass beneath the snow but, still out of Ilinga's sight, he kept a watch on Wurring. Possibly Wurring was only interested in the cave as a shelter.

The twilight came. Everyone seemed tense. Snow started to fall again. Perhaps there was a movement near the mouth of the cave. Then out of the twilight, and just a few minutes before the night closed in, there came a small cloud.

Before he could even push himself under some leafy branches, the cloud of bats was all around him, wings flapping at his face, down his back, and worst of all, flapping at his ears. He tried to get in among the black sallees that grew by the creek, but the bats surrounded him, and their squeaking

83

filled the air. Their wings seemed to be pushing him. One bat even clung to his withers.

Filled with loathing, the iron-grey started to trot downstream, but the bats were thick around him. He broke into a canter, and they still kept with him. In a fury he turned around as though to fight them. This they had not expected, and for a moment they flew past him. Just for a few seconds his vision was clear. He could just make out the group of horses by the stream, then the bats were encircling him again. Perhaps he had only imagined that there was a fourth in the group ... the bats were all around his head, thick, horrible, the smell of them fusty. One clung to his ear. He would shake it off, get rid of them, determine whether someone else had really joined that group by the creek. He stood firm, shaking his head, but the bats clung on, and those on the wing whirled around and around till the air seemed thick with them and their smell.

Just for one second the dark cloud in front of him broke. All was night even without the curtain of wings.... Three ... two half-seen shapes in darkness ... three ... near Wurring? The bats were crowding in again in front of his eyes, settling on him, hooking their claws into him. He began to panic. He screamed with rage and horror, then he could stand it no longer. He could not stay.... Three fillies? But he had to go. His legs began to gallop. He was propelled by fear – and even as he galloped, the bats clung on, and followed, and drove him faster and faster. Nothing he could do would make them leave. He came to a standstill in a few propping strides. He would roll, that might remove them.

The bats that were clinging to his coat and mane freed themselves, but the whole flight of them hovered and waited, coming very close to his waving legs. The horror of them, and their squeaking, and the feel of them made him nearly mad. He got up and galloped and galloped ... and he imagined that the bats were still there, long after they had left him alone ... long after ... long after the falling snow had covered those tracks that had to be made ... long after the snow had hidden a story.

There was trackless snow, when that iron-grey could bear to go back – just the dark night and snow. There was no one to be seen.

For some reason he made straight for the cave mouth. There, he was sure, in the dry cave, out of reach of the snow, he would find something.

All his valley seemed empty, silent, waiting. He hurried to the cave opening.

Eyes watched him in the darkness. Bats waited for him. The only sound was an owl hooting a warning.

* * *

Ilinga had gone out of the cave just on dark, just as the snow began to fall. She went like a shadow across the open grass, barely breathing till she reached the safety of the trees. Then she crept through leaf and branch towards Wurring. She could hear his indrawn breath, knew that his head was up, waiting, wondering. Then her nose was touching his in the darkness.

She felt that there was not a moment to lose. She must lead him to the cave immediately, try to get him over the tumbled boulders, get him away – but he did not move, just stood completely still. The two other fillies came closer, curiously stretching out their own noses to the stranger who had appeared out of the night.

Ilinga waited tensely. If one of them squealed, the iron-grey would probably hear. She did not know where the iron-grey was: he could indeed be quite close. She could feel one of the fillies wrinkling up her nose with excitement. In a moment she would squeal.

Wurring quickly gave the softest nicker to let them know that Ilinga was a friend. Jealousy could still bring great trouble to them. Ilinga felt a swift nip on her shoulder, but there was no sound. Now Wurring *must* move, but he stood. She touched his nose again and took a few steps towards the cave. Still he did not move. She turned round, urged him on. She had seen him hopping, but irrationally she felt that be-

85

cause she had found him, he must be suddenly better.

Wurring began to hop after her on three legs.

It was as though the coldness of winter gripped her, but perhaps he could manage to get through those boulders.

The other two fillies followed also. Ilinga nearly turned round to chase them away, but realized in time that this would only do harm. She knew that a stallion always had more than one mare, and as she felt Wurring near her, she also felt quite certain that she would only to call him, as she had done ever since she was a foal, and he would be hers – perhaps he was hers forever, anyway.

She waited and listened before she stepped out of the last of the trees. She could hear something – a muffled scream of rage. Perhaps it would be wiser to wait for a moment or so, to wait till she knew what was happening. It had sounded like the iron-grey. Then she heard the sound of galloping, pounding hooves that seemed to be going away.

Quickly she led Wurring across the open grass. The two fillies followed. While they were out of the trees the snow fell gently on their backs, their necks. Ilinga felt flakes catching in the long, sensitive hairs of her ears – those hairs that had tingled when she rubbed her head against Wurring's. For a moment she felt almost happy. Wurring was with her: she had found him. Accident, almost more than memory, had led her to the place where she knew he must be – and he was there, and now they were together.

Her feet touched the sand of the cave entrance... softly, softly... and there was no more snow falling on her back. Without thinking she went a little faster, hooves sinking into the sand. Not much further and they would be almost safe, but Wurring could not keep up.

She looked back, waited. Wurring was making a great effort. Even after this small distance and in the cold of falling snow, she could smell his sweat. He *must* get through the boulders. She touched his nose again, her own soft nose moving up his face, encouraging him. When she went on, she did not go so fast, always feeling for Wurring close behind her.

Yet she was so glad at his closeness that she could barely keep her hooves from dancing.

They were into the tunnel: the hard floor would be easier for Wurring. She felt his nose near her flank, but also felt the unevenness of his gait as he hopped on his three sound legs.

Still he kept up – and unfortunately those fillies were close behind him. It had not been in Ilinga's mind that any other filly would be with them. Wurring had not turned them back, so how could she?

In fact Wurring was so torn between happiness at her arrival and anxiety as to how he could possibly escape on three legs, anxiety that the iron-grey should catch Ilinga too, that he had forgotten those fillies even though they had led him to the best grass near water, and often kept him company.

All the way along the smooth floor of the tunnel, he managed to keep up.

Then they came to the boulders. Ilinga climbed over the first few, and they were rough, cold, damp. Immediately the touch of Wurring's nose at her flank was gone. Then she heard his hooves scrabbling on the rocks. He was beside her, gasping for breath. She led on and he followed her painfully over a few more boulders and then there were some that were higher, smoother.

Ilinga found herself sweating too, sweating with fear for Wurring and with knowledge of his pain – and also with desperation. She knew that he could go no further, even before he stopped. She knew he was exhausted by effort and pain. There was still a long way to go through the boulders. He would not be able to do it: she would have to lead him back.

Something told Wurring that she must not go back with them. Everything would be lost, he knew, if she were caught by the iron-grey. Gently he touched her nose, her ears. The softest nicker was the only sound he could allow himself to make ... softly, so softly ... to tell her that she must go, that he would come to her when his shoulder was mended, that she *must* go, or the iron-grey would take her.

Ilinga stood in misery. She could feel Wurring's dejection

87

and also his anxiety. He had to get out of the boulders and out of the cave before the iron-grey found him. Ilinga knew that it would be the end of Wurring if the iron-grey came into the cave and followed their scent into the tunnel while they were still there.

They must go, both of them, each their own way, and quickly. Ilinga was straining her ears for any sound of a horse entering the tunnel. She waited for a moment while Wurring followed the other two fillies over some of the boulders, and then with a feeling of utter desperation, she turned and went back the other way.

By the time she had got through all the boulders, she could hear no sound from the other direction. She was completely alone in the tunnel – and this time she did not have the feeling of going forward to meet Wurring. She had found him, only to have to let him go because he was far too badly hurt to escape with her.

She felt stupid with misery, but she had to hurry. There were other fears in her mind, too. She was not certain that she could get out of the hole into which she had fallen, below that cliff – and she was afraid of the amount of snow that was falling. Then, as she thought of the snow, she wondered what would happen to Wurring if very heavy snow came. She went faster and faster. She had to know if she could get out.

For a little while she forgot any caution: she even trotted along the smooth floor, and the tunnel echoed with the thud of her hooves, the sound filling her head, building up her fear. Fear seemed to beat off the dark walls and the dark roof. She wished the bats would return. Bats could make her nervous sometimes, but these bats were friendly and had helped her so far. Their company would be far better than the company of fear.

She tried to quieten her feet, quieten her own heartbeats, but she only went faster and faster. What stopped her at last was the sudden thought of the tumbled rocks that came quite a long way into the tunnel from the entrance. It would be fatal to race straight into them. She stopped just in time.

In only a few more steps she was feeling her way through the first rocks, and then she was climbing up and over them, finding it all much more difficult, going in this direction, than it had been coming down.

She knew, then, that Wurring could not possibly have got up to the entrance on three legs. At last even she came to one great boulder which she could not climb. She remembered slithering down it, when she came through: now it seemed completely impossible to surmount. She tried over and over again, each time slipping back, each time becoming more exhausted. At last she had to rest – and she had to think. If she could not get up it at all, then she had better get right out of the tunnel and away before daylight. She knew she was getting very hungry.

After she had rested, she tried to find some way around, nervously creeping into cracks, backing out when they started to get at all tight. She thought again of returning to the valley, but what if the iron-grey were already there, already following the scent of her in the cave and in the tunnel?

She must get up the rock. She felt a shelf to one side of it, and a pile-up of boulders. She began to climb – haunches straining . . . and she was up. She stood trembling, but she decided to go a little further on before stopping to rest, just in case that iron-grey came. Surely the big rock would stop him.

It was soon obvious that the worst of the boulders were over. The tunnel was rough, still, but she was sure of being able to make her way to the hole beneath the cliff. She stood, getting her breath. It was then that she heard a sound down the tunnel. All the sweat went cold on her back. Undoubtedly there was a roar of rage, echoing and rolling in the tunnel, magnified a hundred times, till it was terrifying.

She should have gone on, but all she could think of was Wurring. What was happening to Wurring? She waited. There was no other roar, no other sound for a while, and then she could hear a noise of hooves on rock, a rattling noise. After a while that sound stopped. Then there was a roar after roar of fury, deafening reverberations. The big rock must have stopped the iron-grey, at any rate temporarily. She had better go.

After only a few more yards she felt fresh air against her. She must be nearly there. She stumbled over some more rocks, slipped into a pool at the side of the creek. Then there were splashes of spray going all over her. She was there. Round one more rock, and ahead was the last climb. After the pitch darkness of the tunnel at night, it was easier for her to see, and the white rocks caught what light there was.

It did not take long to learn that the final climb, off the sloping bank of mud and up the undercut earth sides of the hole, was perhaps impossible.

After several attempts, each of which finished with her sliding down the wet earth on to the rocks, Ilinga knew she would have to wait till there was a little more light. The more she slid, the more difficult it would be to get up. She stood shivering in the cold spray, her back whitened by the snowflakes that came spiralling down into the hole.

The wind was getting up again. Presently she heard its eerie cry around the cliff above. This was just something else to add to her misery. Wurring was far behind her, now, possibly in danger from that bad-tempered stallion, and she still had to get out of this hole and then, all alone, find somewhere safe to spend the winter.

No horse likes to be alone. Ilinga was very afraid.

12: *A Scent, a Fragrance*

As soon as the iron-grey got near the cave again, the bats flew at him, but before they closed around him he got the faintest whiff of a scent that drove the thought of anything else – even bats – away.

Ilinga had been there, she had gone into the cave. He made a wild rush, shaking his head, trying to drive off those bats. Her scent clung even to the cold sand, even to the walls. There were other scents too – Wurring's and those two fillies. He must, indeed, have seen three fillies with Wurring, under the trees.

He rushed on, following the scent, into the tunnel where he had never dared to go before. He hated bats and he hated to be so enclosed. Now there were bats everywhere, and dark walls pressing close, but he was certain that he was going to find Ilinga, and not even a cloud of bats would stop him.

As the tunnel narrowed he went slower. Even above the smell of the fluttering bats, he could smell the scent of Wurring and the two fillies very strongly. He stopped, his head slightly raised, trying to sort out the various scents. The fragrance of Ilinga was still there, but the other three must be very close.

Then he heard movements. He took a few careful steps forward, and the other sounds stopped. A few more steps, and he was sure he could hear breathing. He moved on through the tunnel, the feeling of being enclosed and the horror of the bats forgotten in the excitement of knowing Ilinga had at last come to his valley.

Something that was not a bat moved up against him. One of the fillies had been unable to stay still when he got really close. He brushed against her, for the tunnel was not very wide.

91

He brushed past the second one, and hurried past Wurring.

There was no one behind Wurring.

This was when the iron-grey roared out his rage, and for a moment the reverbrations of his own roar was terrifying even to himself.

The two fillies' hooves clattered on the stone floor as they leapt away from the noise. Wurring was too lame and sore to jump away.

The iron-grey walked on. Ilinga's scent was there but so much overlayed by that of the others that he knew that they must have left her further along – or she had gone on while they came back. He would lose her after all, if he did not hurry.

He started to trot, then all of a sudden he was among boulders, he was on his knees, his nose crashed into a large rock. As he got up, he screamed with fury . . . but there was Ilinga's scent again.

He picked his way carefully over the heaps of rocks. The scent of the other three was still there. The rocks got higher and rougher. Then there was only Ilinga's scent. She had gone on without them – and not long ago.

Where she had gone, he would go too. Now he would catch up with her.

Slipping and stumbling, climbing, falling, he followed where Ilinga had passed not very long before.

He came to the enormous rock. Here he could smell her as though she were still there. The scent was so strong that it called up the whole picture of her – every lovely line, the thrilling grace of her carriage, dark head held proudly, neck arched, and the mane that seemed to hold such unusual lights, the supple back, the curve of the quarters, the proud-held tail – all, all Ilinga was there in his mind, except the flesh and the gay and lovely spirit of her, the unobtainable and beautiful.

He began to try to find a way over this rock. It seemed to block the whole tunnel – but the scent was all around him. For a moment he wondered giddily if she were there, somewhere hidden. He explored around, putting his head into every crevice, following in with his shoulders if he fitted. Around, behind the rock, the scent was so strong that he followed unwisely far, and his shoulders became stuck. He wriggled and became more tightly wedged. He began to scream with fear, pushed with his feet and, scraping his shoulders, slid out backwards, still roaring.

For a while he attacked the rock without stopping to think out any way of climbing it. Then he began to try to work out how Ilinga must have got over it. Between each attempt he rested and felt around for footholds.

Ilinga had got up it somehow. He was so anxious to find her that he did not get bad-tempered over failing to climb the rock – he just kept on trying. Hours passed, and if it had not been for Ilinga's scent, he would have given up in fury, and rushed down to work off his bad temper by finishing Wurring. Even the bats must have decided he would not be able to get up because most of them left him alone.

Something told him that it must be almost morning. If Ilinga had a way of escaping out of this tunnel, he had better get up the rocks quickly, or he might never catch her.

This time he made a prodigious leap, struggled with all his strength – and made it.

Ilinga's scent called him on and on over the boulders, but soon there was moving air, fresh air coming in. He crashed and scrambled over the rocks, hurrying stupidly. Suddenly he was falling and there was fire burning in his off knee. The leg was gripped between boulders, and it was twisting as he fell, twisting, twisting. He wrenched it out, and struggled to his feet, then he went madly on. Faint light was seeping into the tunnel. He must be coming to the end. He would find Ilinga very soon. With this air coming in, the scent did not hang so strongly.

He slithered into a pool, fell again, picked himself up, barely noticing that his leg was becoming less and less steady.

Ilinga had passed by these rocks beside him. He forced himself forward over the last boulders into the half light.

A brown filly with proud head held up listening – this was

what he would see. A brown filly that he had won at last.

The hole was empty and there was only the slightest lingering fragrance.

He looked round wildly. There were her hoofmarks on the sloping slab of mud, lots of hoofmarks, signs of her having jumped. There were also the marks of scrabbling, struggling hind legs. These were being washed away by the water because they were just where the creek poured over the earth lip into the deep hole.

He stood staring at it all. He sprang out on to the sloping wedge of mud. Suddenly the pain in his knee gripped him. He tried to leap from this mud towards the creek, and crashed down right into the water and on to the rocks. For a moment the creek poured over him.

Flashes of pain went up from his knee, making him quite stupid. One last grain of sense remained. He must get back down the tunnel before he became too stiff.

He got up and began to work his way downwards again, his temper getting worse as the pain increased and as his feeling of frustration grew stronger.

When he reached the opening of the cave, the young horses had vanished, and the snow was falling, falling.

*   *   *

Ilinga had waited till daylight came, and the fear had been with her all through those hours that the iron-grey had followed her and would suddenly appear out of the dark tunnel.

When daylight came, she knew she had to get out, or wait till night time and go back to the iron-grey's valley. The sides of the hole looked hopelessly difficult.

She studied the sides, working out a possible way up. From the sloping lump of earth to a jutting-out rock might be done with a good jump. Then she would have to turn a little and make a tremendous leap for the one place where the side of the hole was broken down by the stream.

She balanced on the slippery earth, braced herself, and

95

sprang. She made the rock, but wavered back and forth, shoulder touching the cold earth, and then swaying away from it, straining to hold on with her hooves, straining to balance. Better to jump back than to fall. She landed on the wet lump of earth, slid, and managed to remain standing. She looked up. This time she would not try to stay on that rock: just jump on to it, turning in mid-air, land and jump again before falling.

She leapt, twisting, felt the rock under her hooves, and pushed off in another big spring, extending her forefeet at the last minute, to try to get a grip of the wet earth. Her hind feet slipped. She was struggling to get a toehold. Then there was something firm underneath her near hind hoof: her off hoof got a hold too. She heaved herself up.

She was there! Standing in the creek above the hole, wet with the freezing water, streaming with sweat from effort and fear. She was up, and in the light, in the snow, even touched by the wind.

Then she noticed the depth of the snow all around her. Here was the next danger to fear, snow, snow, snow. Snow was still falling steadily – and she was alone.

She stood there, in that deep cleft valley, below the cliff, below the tall mountain ash with their snow-spattered bark and their towering heads covered. She was gasping for breath, and with each gulp of cold air it was as if she tried to draw in strength and wisdom – for what should she do now? Where should she go?

The snow began to fall faster. Her longing to go home to Numeramang would have to be forgotten. There was too much high country to cross. Her bones would bleach up there. How should she get down lower?

She turned up the ridge on the opposite side to that which she had slipped down.

13: *Wraiths in the Blizzard*

The snow lay thickly and unmarked. Ilinga slipped and slid
her way up the steep side of the valley. The wild raspberry
was already getting covered with snow, wattle trees were

bowed down. White snow and trees bounded her vision, and when she reached the top of the ridge all she could see were the blowing snow and the trees. Then suddenly she stopped in mid-stride. There was something, marks, disturbed snow... signs of a horse and fresh tracks leading up the ridge.

She stood for a minute, her eyes searching for the shape of this horse in among the trees – but there were only the hoof-marks, and the snow falling into them, filling them up, covering them over. She moved forward, head down, sniffing at the tracks.

Had he waited all that time? But after all she had only been in that tunnel for two nights. It was the young brown stallion, of that she was sure, and he was on his own. The bay from Ravine must have gone back.

Ilinga was too lonely and too afraid to feel anything but a sudden warmth of friendship for that young brown horse, and she followed his tracks quite fast. She must not let the tracks get covered by the fast-falling snow. While she could see them, she did not feel so alone. Also it was possible that he knew the way to warmer, low country where there would be grass. She was very hungry.

She had not been following for more than ten minutes when she saw him ahead, jogging along through the trees. He did look as if he knew where he was going, yet he had first appeared, days ago now, somewhere near Ravine, so he must be quite a long way from his own country. Ilinga slowed her pace. As long as she did not lose sight of him, all would be well. She was not at all sure that she wanted to catch up with him right away – not even in the depths of a snow storm.

The brown horse ahead of her threaded his way through the tall tree trunks – brown horse cloaked by the clouds of falling snow; young beautiful horse, young beautiful filly following him, the two of them like wraiths passing through the storm. The brown stallion did not know that Ilinga was behind him, though she, and she alone, had held him waiting there, above the vanishing river.

If it had been Wurring ahead he would have felt her presence, for some flashing sympathy existed between those two.

The snow fell down, thick and fast. Tracks were covered soon. A stronger gust of wind whirled the flakes in a twisting cloud. Ilinga lost sight of the brown horse for a few seconds, and his tracks were barely visible. She broke into a canter, swishing past some low wattles, so that the snow exploded off their branches. She must not lose him. For a while she had not been alone, and now she was alone again, while she could not see him.

It was completely urgent not to lose him.

Snow beat in her eyes. Then she saw him moving ahead, and she hurried, going even a little closer this time, so that she would not lose him again.

The snow fell thicker and thicker. The brown horse vanished again. Ilinga shot forward, afraid, so afraid that this time she might be blown off course and not find him at all. It was so easy to get lost in snow, in great white clouds of beating snowflakes.

There he was, and she trotted closer and closer, so that only the wildest of blizzards could make him become invisible.

In forest country, a blizzard cannot become as dense, as suffocating, as twisting as it does on the open mountain tops, but this storm eventually became a tremendous blizzard through which it was nearly impossible to keep going.

The two browns became white with snow, so that there was never the full outline of two horses trotting on through the trees. Ilinga came up almost head to quarters with the young horse. She thought he must have known, then, that she was there, but his whole mind and effort was on one thing, on getting safely out of the blizzard. When he did not turn round to look at her, she began to wonder if he did know she was there, or if he thought he were dreaming.

In this ghostly companionship they trotted on and on, along the top of a narrow ridge which went for miles, and where, even though there were trees, the wind came with a hurtle and crash, and the snow whirled thick and fast. They passed shadowy trees that were plastered with snow – or through trees that

99

they could not see at all. They went on and on, snow beating in their eyes, wind pushing them off the ridge in stronger and stronger gusts, snow falling, falling, making them dizzy.

Ilinga stumbled. Her nose nearly touched the off side of the young brown stallion's quarters, actually brushed some of the snow off it. This time he did turn his head, and his eyes, all fringed with snow, looked unbelieving. He kept on trotting, but he turned his head again, looked once more. This time he stopped, sniffed at her head, still unbelieving. To Ilinga it was almost as though she were not there.

For days she had thought of nothing but how to find Wurring, and then how to get him away from the iron-grey. The young brown stallion had only thought how he might win Ilinga's attention: now this was all changed. The most important thing for both young horses was to get out of the snow and survive.

Slowly Ilinga began to feel that she really existed for the young horse. Then the blizzard did not seem to blow so strongly, because there were the two of them to fight their way through it.

Then the ridge began to drop a little. The trees got thinner. The wind seemed almost strong enough to lift them and carry them away. The trees ended, and ahead there was just swirling snow, no solid world in which to set their hooves, nothing to tell them which way they should go. Open country and the wild blizzard would engulf them.

Ilinga began to wonder if the brown stallion really did know where he was travelling. He stopped on the edge of the trees, looking at the white world beyond. The sound of the wind filled the air, and yet there seemed to be a sort of silence. Not a bird cried. Every other living creature except the two young horses must have been huddled in safety, in thick trees, or hollows. Their aloneness was immense. Even the cry of a currawong would have made the world less vast and unfriendly.

The snow would surely be falling in the iron-grey's valley, too, and how would Wurring make for lower country fast enough?

100

The brown stallion started off through the whirling clouds of snow. Ilinga had to keep her head right to his flank, or she would have lost him. The battle for her own safety was too great to allow her to wonder much about how Wurring would stay alive.

Snow filled the air they breathed. The bitter, snow-filled wind drove them, buffeted them, blew them always in one direction – off the course which the brown horse tried to keep.

If the wind blew them apart for even a second, Ilinga's fear became blind terror. The force of the blizzard had become too great for them to trot across it. They walked, and she kept her shoulder pressed to his flank. The journey was endless. The beating, twisting, wind-swivelled snow was their world, world without end. Once, the young brown horse stopped and flung an agonized neigh to the snow-filled sky. The snow muffled the sound that would usually have carried for miles. No one would have heard it, there was none to answer.

They went on, leaning against the blizzard, blinded and breathless – and perhaps lost. On they went – one brown leg, all spattered with snow, after the other, one hoof stepping into white space and then another, step after step into cold snow, step after step.

There was something darker ahead.

They passed under one lone tree and then there were trees on either side and soon they were going down hill. The young brown stallion quickened his pace, and Ilinga kept beside him, shoulder to flank. She could tell by the way he relaxed that he must be fairly certain that they were coming to safety.

She was so tired. She just kept on trotting with her head to his flank. Sometime this white, whirling world must come to an end, and they would have grass underfoot again. Slowly it all became a vast, moving blur of falling snow.

They began to drop downwards more steeply, and soon they were becoming sheltered from the worst of the wind. Some of the snow fell off their coats. They were horses again, not ghosts in a blizzard, and they could see out of their eyes.

It was necessary to keep going, though, in case the blizzard

101

increased and the snow became deep, far down the mountains.

Ilinga was quite exhausted by the time they had gone down to that level where the snow became pouring rain.

It was almost dark when the young brown stallion stopped trotting, and dropped his head to graze. Ilinga no longer felt hungry, only deeply tired. She went to sleep on her feet beside him, and, if he moved, woke up only enough to move close to him. Soon he slept too.

*   *   *

The young brown stallion looked at her curiously. She was hollow-flanked, exhausted. She had obviously been looking for someone ... where had she vanished to when she fell? What had happened, and how had she come back?

He shook the rain out of his coat. Winter had really come, and winter was a time of struggle. It was also a time to hear of great mysteries.

The valley into which he had led Ilinga held a number of horses. There was fairly good grass. It was the valley in which his sire's herd had always wintered. His sire and dam were there, and other stallions, other mares, many young horses. There was room for them all. In spring they would part up into smaller herds. Then there might be a fight or so for mares, but now all was peaceful. There were other things to think about than fighting. Food and shelter would be most important during all the winter months.

The young brown horse knew that Ilinga would run with him all winter, but he had a strong feeling that she was possessed by someone else, absolutely possessed, or else why had she run from him?

14: *Hop, Hop or Die*

Wurring and the two fillies left the mouth of the cave very
quickly, but Wurring did not want to go far away. Only if the
iron-grey came out again, alone, would he be sure that Ilinga
had got away. So he waited and waited, knowing that if the

iron-grey came out disappointed, and found him standing there, he would probably be killed. He pressed himself right into thick branches and leaves and hoped that he would not be seen. The fillies were afraid and, for the first time, left him.

He waited and waited.

He waited and the cold snow fell. If only he had had the strength to go off with Ilinga. Suddenly it seemed that he must gallop off through the snow, feel strong again, and young, and race the blizzard with his beautiful filly – the lovely one who had run with him from the time she was a motherless foal.

As the snow fell, ceaselessly, like an ever-moving curtain, he remembered some of the strange tales that had sounded through the bush ever since that night when Ilinga's dam had followed Winganna and the other two mares into the great flat at Numeramang – the tales of something that had happened years and years ago, or something that absolutely had to happen. And, as he stood in the falling snow, the air seemed electric, thrilling. He was tingling, like he tingled when his hair and Ilinga's touched, and the stories were alive in the air around him – a mare of the moonlight breed, a stallion that was full of the fire of the sun ... the impossible union of sun and moon over glittering snow. Even as the excitement shook him, so that he had forgotten where he was, forgotten that there was anything but glory, that which had been in the brolga's dance came to him – a warning – of danger, danger, and of the almost complete vanishing of the sun. Then, indeed, the snow fell cold on his back.

Wurring waited, and all night long the wind would spiral the snow around and sigh: 'Vanish, vanish, the sun may vanish.'

At last there seemed to be faint shreds of light in the sky – snowflakes bearing light danced in front of his eyes. If the iron-grey did not soon come ... Fear for Ilinga was like a fox creeping through the bushes.

If the iron-grey did catch her, he would certainly bring her back to his own valley. Wurring would know what had happened.

Just before the dawn really came, some bats flew out,

seemed to search around for something, and then came towards Wurring's hiding place. They fluttered in among the leaves, quietly around his head. A feeling of well-being went through him. All was not lost. . . .

Far away a dingo howled and its mate answered. The world went on. All was not lost.

Daylight had become stronger, and Wurring could see how heavily the snow was falling. Then the iron-grey appeared in the sandy cave.

He, too, was on three legs – and he was alone.

Wurring looked at him in amazement. It did not really matter how he had got hurt. Ilinga had got away and somehow the iron-grey had been lamed, and Wurring had nothing really to fear from him for a while.

The iron-grey stood in the sandy cave. He stood and he stood, and he watched the snow. Wurring suddenly knew, as the snow poured down around him too, that what he had to fear, now, was just the snow.

In case it kept on falling, and did not melt all winter, he should start to go down lower. It would take him a long time to get far, particularly if the snow got very deep. The iron-grey still stood there. Wurring did not wish to be seen so he waited a minute or so, then the iron-grey hopped a few yards: he was very lame. It was obvious he was no danger at present, but he might be some use, he might know where grass for the winter would be found.

A big gust of wind lifted the snow off the ground, and swirled the falling snow densely. Everything was blotted out in a blinding white cloud. Wurring quickly backed away, putting quite a number of trees between him and the iron-grey while the cloud hid him. When the cloud cleared, the iron-grey had moved too. It was time to follow him downstream, and Wurring could just see him, hopping down the valley; see his tracks being quickly filled with snow.

Wurring crossed the creek and began to hop down on the opposite side from the iron-grey, a little behind him and hidden in trees.

As the snow storm got heavier and heavier, the situation was becoming desperate for both lame horses. They had to beat the snow or die. The grass would all be buried, and no horse on three legs could hop far through very deep snow. They must beat the snow now, before it lay too thickly.

Hop, hop, hop, or die. Hop, hop, hop, or die. Blinding cold snow beat in Wurring's eyes, plastered his back.

Great danger . . . There had been great danger from the iron-grey. Now there was great danger from the winter's snow, but the strange thing was that very soon the snowflakes that slid past his ears only whispered of a moonlight-coloured mare – not of the extinguished sun's light, nor of death and danger. Wurring may have started off feeling that every hop was an effort, and that if he did not get away from the heavy snow he would die, but before he had been going for long, the future seemed to be thrilling. He remembered last winter, when he and Ilinga and the other young horses had galloped so gaily through the snow. Did he remember all the legends too, or were they going to sound all this winter as they had last winter – in the tinkle of ice on snowgum leaves, in the cry of the wind?

Wurring was suddenly in another world, a world where the iron-grey was no longer of such importance. As the falling snow whispered to him, he did not mind that he was on three legs. Before the snow was gone he would race over it, flinging up the silver spray behind him. He would assuredly go to Ilinga, when the blizzards allowed him to. He tossed his head, suddenly wild with joy – even though he still hopped, even though the first heavy snows fell and there was all the winter still ahead. Joy made the fire of the invisible sun burn through him.

Ilinga had come, had found him – this was all that mattered. Pain did not matter. He would be better before the snows had gone.

The wind cried of the sun and the moon. The wind's winter cry that could mean death was full of an old story of life.

Wurring did not realize that he had started going faster till

106

he saw he had caught up with the iron-grey, who was just across the creek from him. He had better slow down. He was counting on the older horse leading him to a place of safety where there would be grass to eat while the blizzards raged.

The iron-grey had not noticed him.

Wurring suddenly saw that there were quite a few tracks in the snow in front of the other stallion. The herd must have gone ahead. He wondered if the two fillies were with them, or behind.

All over the mountains there would be horses making down, and kangaroos and wallabies – if they had not already gone. For a while the roar of the wind, the cry of black cockatoos, and the song of the currawongs would be all that sounded over the white mountain-tops. When the blizzard ceased to blow and the sun shone again there would be the curve of snow against the sky and no moving animal to track it except perhaps a hare – and nobody knows where the hare goes.

The day was growing later, darker. They were hopping on and on down the river. There was still snow falling and much snow underfoot. Wurring knew he was getting tired. He had crossed two or three little creeks, and others had come in from the opposite side. The stream was becoming quite large, the valley wide.

The iron-grey stopped underneath a big tree and started nosing around for grass. Wurring stopped too. Perhaps the older stallion knew it was safe to stop here and rest . . . but that big, heavy horse looked exhausted. . . . Wurring decided he would not stop, but keep going down the river – and just hope that the valley did not become a gorge. The tracks of the rest of the herd still went on. He would cross the stream presently, on to the iron-grey's side, and go where the herd had gone: their tracks would be company.

He was very tired, but a burning desire for life kept him going. If he could get to good grass for the winter, the future would blaze ahead – there would be no death in darkness and deep snow.

107

Sometimes he was so burning with a feeling of urgency, that he put his lame leg to the ground and barely noticed the pain. Wurring was starting to recover, even though by late at night, when he found the herd down where the snow barely lay at all, he was totally exhausted.

Wurring slept under a tree near some of the old, wise mares. If the snow came more heavily, and they moved, he would wake up and go with them.

In the morning it was only rain that fell, but, by the clouds, snow still fell heavily, higher up. Was Ilinga up there? Wurring felt certain that she would have made down somehow.

Two more days and the rain had stopped. Perhaps it still snowed up there ... Whether it had stopped or not, a lot of snow must have fallen. Somewhere, when the sun shone, there would be peaks glistening against the sky.

Wurring searched around for food. There were some bushes whose leaves and seedpods satisfied his hunger more than anything else did, bushes that in summer had a pea-shaped flower. These grew some distance up a little creek where, when the sun was out, it was mild and warm. No one else seemed to bother to go there.

The iron-grey had come down the valley, but his leg was horribly swollen. The pain made his temper even worse than usual, but since he could not gallop after anyone, and could not kick, it did not matter. No one went close enough to be bitten.

The two fillies arrived too, and were as restless as all the others of the herd, old and young. Perhaps it was because the stallion, whom they disliked, was hurt, and they had the feeling that they might escape. The valley of the caves was a good home, but since the iron-grey had destroyed their old and beloved stallion, life had not been happy.

As the days passed, Wurring's shoulder began to improve and, though he had a thick winter coat, it was a good colour, and his mane and tail were good too. He found he could use his leg for walking, then he could even trot a little. The leaves and the seedpods were good, healing food. He never went near

108

to the iron-grey, but one day he trotted past him by mistake and saw the older stallion eyeing him rather thoughtfully.

Wurring stopped and looked at his lame enemy. Perhaps by the end of the winter the iron-grey might not be the strongest.

Who cared? Wurring did not wish to fight. He only wished to search the mountains for Ilinga and then to gallop, gay and free, with her.

Some mare or filly in the herd started the feeling that went through them all, the feeling that the iron-grey was done and that Wurring would take over. It might have been the most handsome of the two fillies, the brown one, for she was a mischief maker.

Wurring felt this, and saw the herd appraising him, and, though he felt stronger and better each day, and it would only need the spring for life to surge through him, something told him that the iron-grey was not finished yet, something told him: 'Danger, danger. The light of the sun will go.'

15: *Darkness on the Midday Mountains*

Though most of Winganna's herd had gone down the Tumut River, they had eventually made their way back to Ravine and Numeramang. They were leaderless, and this is unusual because a winning stallion usually takes a herd. The iron-grey had only taken one filly – and lost her. None of them knew that he had maimed Wurring and taken him, after losing Ilinga.

Yarran had had Wurring and Ilinga run with her for so long that she missed them and kept expecting them to come out of the bush, also her foal had died.

When the winter snow began to fall – so early, so heavy – it was she who led the horses away from Numeramang, and she led them to Ravine, because this was the way Wurring and Ilinga had gone. Ravine would probably be free of snow, but she had no intention of staying with the Ravine stallion when the spring time came. Then would come a time to wander the mountains until she heard some wild, thrilling call, or saw some stallion that was worthy to be her mate – for Yarran was a beautiful mare. Now she was not thinking of springtime – she was wondering most about Wurring and Ilinga. She remembered that the iron-grey was a savage, ill-tempered horse.

Snow did fall in Ravine, feathering with white the plum-coloured cliffs, but it did not lie except in the shadowed, roofless rooms of the mud-brick buildings. The horses had nothing to fear. The grass was not covered for more than an hour or so.

Yarran and the small herd came down to Ravine as the snow was falling, and because of the dense drift of flakes, no one

110

took much notice of them — and then, when the snow stopped, they were there, and everyone was used to seeing them.

The wind blew the snow round and round in the valley and voices were in the wind — snow voices, wind voices, and the remembered echo of the brolgas' crying at another time.

Yarran was not long in Ravine before she knew that both Wurring and Ilinga had been seen there, and that the iron-grey had come in the most furious temper. Something had happened to Wurring. She even knew that the bay stallion had gone after Ilinga – but he had returned alone. She learnt that the way he had gone was through the high, rolling country where the snow lay all winter: he had come back through the start of the blizzard. It seemed that something strange had happened. Even the stolid bay horse was disturbed by whatever it was that had come to pass.

A few days went by. No one worried the new horses that had recently arrived. The snow began to melt even in between the thick mud walls. A wind blew, shimmering the snowgum leaves to silver, and Yarran knew that Ilinga had vanished in a mysterious way, a way that was not to be understood at all.

Yarran was filled with curiosity as to what had happened – and she was missing both Wurring and Ilinga very much. All these things she had learnt about them stayed in her mind during the winter, and they blended with the old bush legends that had been in the air ever since Ilinga's dam walked into Numeramang. Wurring was the sun – but in all the herds of wild horses, over seasons and seasons uncounted, there had sometimes been born these chestnuts who burnt with the sun's life.

The breed of the moon, the legends went, had silver moonlight through their hair.

As the winter went on, she learnt of a wide valley through which the Tumut River ran, not so very much further down, and where many horses wintered, but she had it in her mind that both Wurring and Ilinga were far to the east where both sun and moon rise, or she might have tried going down there. To go to the east was impossible, now the snow had come.

The bay stallion had not settled down, Yarran noticed. He was nervous. Whenever snow fell, he moved round ceaselessly, as though expecting something to happen. Day after day the feeling grew among all the horses that something was going to happen. Then one bright winter's day, when the sun glittered on the snow-capped hills, every horse seemed to know that sometime, quite soon, the light of the sun would go.

How could they believe it when the sunlight streamed gold

and silver fire on the snow, but they did believe it. All the animals of the bush were restless, too. The currawongs cried the legend aloud, and when the storms came, the black cockatoos called of darkness. At night the howl of the dingos told the same story. All the bush was waiting.

Then a blizzard darkness came – the sort of darkness that everyone knew – and more snow and more rain fell. For a while the stories could sound unheard, while the search for food was the most important thing.

*   *   *

Lower down the Tumut River the same tale echoed in every bird call. Even the harsh bark of the flying phallangers held a warning of darkness.

Often Ilinga would start upwards, hoping the snow had gone, only to find, after she had ploughed through a mile or so of soft snow, that her way became blocked by the white and gleaming hills, and she would have to return, each time feeling more desperately that Wurring must be in danger, or perhaps stranded somewhere in the snow, dying of hunger.

The weeks went on, and Ilinga became more and more restless – and indeed the other horses were too. Heavy rain came, pouring down, beating the dead leaves into the ground, glistening on the rocks. The river rose.

Then there was warm sunshine, and Ilinga started forth again, and this time found fresh snow even lower than before.

She stood staring at the bright white hills, rolling away against the blue sky, higher and higher, and knew, as she let the urge to climb them go rushing through her, that she herself was growing stronger as the weather turned towards spring. The grass had been good, and the Tumut Valley was warm already.

She rolled in the snow to remove some of her winter coat, took one last look at the gleaming mountains which separated her from Wurring, and started down again. A clear pool of water lay where a little creek flowed over a hollow rock. She stopped to drink. There was a filly looking at her again – a different filly with strands of silver in mane and forelock.

Ilinga, startled, looked over her shoulder, but no one was there. Had a moon filly been behind her? No, there was no one else but herself. Who could she be?

The young brown stallion was watching out for her as she arrived back. Sometime soon she would have to leave, and leave in the night so that she just vanished and he would not know where she had gone.

That night the warm wind of spring started to blow.

*　　*　　*

Wurring's valley was getting warmer too, and Wurring, himself, was strong. His shoulder was mended. Here, also, the future was cried aloud by the wind through the rocks, so that all those who heard would shiver, and then the liquid spring song of the thrush would make all the beauty of moonlight and sunlight blend together, making it true, so true, that happiness must come again.

For days a warm wind blew, and then there was rain and the river came down, swift and fast. It was brown with mud, and it carried logs and branches. Spring had come.

After the rain, the sun shone. It shone, warm and wonderful, on Wurring's coat. He bucked and reared, and galloped round, thinking how wonderful he felt and that he would find Ilinga soon. His coat was beginning to shine, and his magnificent mane and tail – silver, or gold, or simply sunlight – made every horse look at him.

Unfortunately this magnificence made the iron-grey look too. Wurring may have had no thought of fighting, but the iron-grey, older and heavier – his leg still not as well healed as Wurring's – only felt fierce anger and jealousy at the admiration the young horse got from the mares.

So the iron-grey waited his chance – or just waited and watched.

Three days after the rain, when the river had dropped

114

again, Wurring started off upstream. He was so tense with expectation of some strange happening that he could not have stayed still. Every horse was tense. Even the birds were quieter, having called for so long that darkness would come, and the sun vanish.

The iron-grey followed.

Twenty-four hours later, in darkness, Ilinga left the Tumut Valley, and the young brown stallion did not know she had left till morning.

*　　*　　*

Wurring followed the river back up towards the valley of the caves, and he walked with springing strides, or he trotted. Once where the ground was flat and open, he broke into a bouncing, bucking canter, and the sunlight blazed in his hair.

The iron-grey had some trouble to keep up, but he was close enough to see this exhibition of joy and vigour – also beauty – and his jealousy smouldered all the more.

They were coming to quite a large open flat, and he determined to catch up, there, and finish Wurring off. He hurried, but Wurring had heard him and was not bothering about him, and just went cantering on, kicking up his heels rather disdainfully. The iron-grey was too out of breath to get round in front of him. Wurring kept purposefully trotting. They covered the ground a lot quicker than they had when they were driven down by the snow. The iron-grey found it hard work, the knee was still quite sore.

He did not catch up with Wurring all day.

It was evening when they reached the valley of the caves. Here there was still some patches of soggy snow left, and many solid snow banks that would stop quick travelling. Wurring was feeling full of strength still, and he was tired of the iron-grey always following. He decided to hide in a cave, wait till the iron-grey came, and then fight him.

It was a few minutes or so before the iron-grey came into sight, and he was lame and blowing. Even so, he looked far stronger and heavier than Wurring knew he was himself.

Wurring did not spring out. Perhaps it might be better to stop the night there? But some instinct told him that he should fight the iron-grey while he was lame and tired. Night . . . darkness . . . danger. Better to fight him now. Wurring came out of the cave. The iron-grey was still pounding up the valley, thinking he was ahead.

Wurring leapt after him, his hooves almost soundless on the wet sand. The iron-grey only heard him at the last moment, and swung around, with barely time to steady himself.

The iron-grey had fought before. Wurring knew this, but Wurring had learnt some wisdom in the last few months. He had the most speed, he was much more nimble. If he kept out of reach until he could get in a really good blow, he might never win, but he might not be hurt this time.

Presently he realized that he could drive the iron-grey nearly mad, by simply dancing out of reach, and it was great fun to do this, but the very smell of the heavy horse reminded him that this was a cruel, bad-tempered animal. Wurring did not think – even if he managed to exhaust him – that he would have the strength to kill the iron-grey . . . yet. He had to kill him sometime, to avenge Winganna.

He would play safe now, while night closed in. Try to exhaust the bigger horse, then leave him. But Wurring got tired too, and when he found himself tiring, he decided to draw off and see if the iron-grey followed.

The grey horse had had enough for the night, but he did start to follow upstream, so Wurring decided that he might as well rest. The morning would be another day.

The morning was indeed another day. A few clouds floated over the sky, dark-based, lazy, presaging rain. For some reason both horses were nervous. The day was unusually hot. There was also a frightening feeling of hurry and constant movement in the bush. Wurring was afraid to go on his way, because he was certain something vast was going to happen – and he did not know what.

The iron-grey did not disturb him, though he kept a careful

watch on the younger horse. They both grazed half-heartedly, both kept watching the lazy clouds, kept sniffing the air.

All the other animals that Wurring saw were furtive, and scuttling along as though really afraid of something. He saw a dark brown wallaby hopping through undergrowth and it stopped often to point its trembling nose up towards the sky. Then it vanished. The birds were quiet: there was no joyous carolling, only a few necessary calls for communication. What worried him most was when he saw two snakes – and then a third – making up on to the ridge above the stream. They, too, seemed in a hurry. Wurring felt profoundly uncomfortable.

He did not move off until almost mid-day, when he felt quite unable to stay still amid the tension he could feel in the bush and in the weather. Any animals which he saw were still going fast and some were looking over their shoulders. The hot, lazy wind came in puffs, turning the snowgum leaves to glittering silver. Puff! and then the wind would die down so that the leaves hung quite still and were olive green again and there was no sigh of bark or branch. Something was certainly going to happen, and he could not bear to wait any longer to see what it was.

He moved off up the valley, and the iron-grey immediately followed, almost immediately began to canter up alongside.

Wurring had no intention of running away. He knew he could keep out of reach of the big lame horse. As he swung round to fight, he forgot all his foreboding about the day, forgot the scurrying animals, the birds who did not sing, the snakes that slid swiftly through the bush. He remembered the iron-grey, and he remembered Ilinga, too, and Winganna, because there are some great reasons for fighting – a horse fights for a mare, or a herd, or he fights for vengeance. Wurring was fighting for his mare, and to avenge his sire – he was also fighting for his own life.

The day grew more and more sultry, and the sweat streamed on the older horse, who was striking out with venom and force, and it darkened the coat of the young, gleaming chestnut.

Wurring kept hopping gracefully out of reach, and aiming his own blows infrequently and only when he got an opportunity to hit at the most vulnerable places.

Today, however, was indeed another day. Whatever made it so oppressive affected Wurring rather more than it did the more stolid horse. For Wurring the day was becoming nerve-wracking: the iron-grey had not noticed all the signs that something strange was going to happen: his whole attention was towards maiming Wurring again. Half of Wurring's attention was feeling for something in the weather – in the day itself.

The iron-grey got in one stinging blow on Wurring's shoulder; the same shoulder which he had hurt before. It was painful for a moment, but no real damage had been done, and it did serve the purpose of making the young horse more careful. Wurring reared away from the blow and brought his own forefeet crashing down on the iron-grey's head.

On and on the fight went. Two horses swaying back and forth. By now there seemed even more hasty movement of animals through the bush. Two big kangaroos were hopping in great leaps down the valley. While Wurring's attention was partly distracted by the kangaroos, the iron-grey came for him. Wurring got a dizzying blow on the head before he knew what was happening. He shook his head, but everything looked a little dark. He realized that the kangaroos had become as still as tree stumps among some rocks, and that there was no more rustling, only complete, deathly silence in the bush.

The iron-grey came rushing at him again. Wurring stepped swiftly aside. The world might look dark, but he was not unsteady on his feet. He felt quite clear in his head. The iron-grey sprang at him again. This time Wurring jumped away and aimed a considerable slash at the other's eye, missed the eye, itself, but drew blood from above it.

Everything seemed even darker. Wurring cast an anxious glance at the sky – for it appeared as if night were coming and yet it was mid-day, he was sure. As he looked up, the infuriated grey stallion, with blood running into his eye, sprang.

118

One blow stupified Wurring for long enough to allow the iron-grey to strike him again. Wurring had to collect himself quickly, to get out of the way, and his head was spinning.

The whole valley was even darker.

He succeeded in keeping out of reach, and with every moment, his head cleared, but the darkness was even more noticeable.

He saw the iron-grey give a wild look around him...He must have noticed the darkness too...Then, as though he believed that the dark was being caused by the cut Wurring had given him above the eye, the grey stallion came hurtling in to fight with all his strength.

Wurring was sure that the iron-grey had seen that it was becoming dark, so it was not just he imagining that night was coming in the middle of the day! Surely the scuttling animals had known something. The sun was gone when it should be high in the sky. On a clear day the light of the sun was vanishing...

He jumped out of the iron-grey's reach, and only got half the blow that was aimed at him, but the bigger stallion was furious.

Could it be that Wurring was to die as the sun's light was extinguished?

Wurring could get away if he turned and galloped, he knew, but the darkness was unnatural and terrifying. He could not gallop into it, but he kept moving up the valley as they fought.

No sun was there to make his mane foam with light. The day had turned to night almost completely.

The iron-grey was screaming with rage – and perhaps with terror. Flailing hooves were all around Wurring, but he did not turn and run...not into the dark...and this horse had to be beaten....Or was he going to be beaten himself?

Darkness settled down on the mid-day mountains.

16: *A Great Swirling Pool*

After the first warm wind, the first warm rains, Yarran left
Ravine. She knew that it would still be impossible to go directly east because there would be deep, packed snow, so she
made downwards and to the north, first intending, later, to try
to cut across the mountains in an easterly direction.

She did not wish to stay near the bay stallion of Ravine,

now that spring was starting. She had no wish to be one of his herd, and it would be interesting to see what herds, what stallions, were lower down the Tumut. Wildfire was burning through her. She longed to gallop over high, open country with some stallion as wonderful as Winganna, if one such existed. Somewhere soon, there would be a wild call ringing out, perhaps ringing over snow, for her. She would answer it, but before this she had to find Wurring and Ilinga. She had to be certain that Wurring survived the immense danger which she knew threatened him.

She picked her way round steep sidelings above the Tumut River; handsome mare threading through the tall white ribbon-gums and the rough-barked peppermints. Occasionally her hooves brushed through the purple of easy-flowering sarsa-parilla. Sometimes the sarsaparilla crept all over a bush, splashing its colour above the rocks.

Yarran went on steadily, glad that she had managed to leave Ravine without the bay noticing. Lower down there were even bacon-and-egg bushes flowering – golden and velvety brown. The going became easier, and after a while she could see below her the valley opening out, wide and green, and many horses were dotted about.

She walked down, quietly, and keeping hidden in trees, but she walked with proud bearing, as befitted a mare who was beautiful and who had much wisdom. When she reached the fringe of the trees, she did not go into the clear country, but wandered round the edge of it, looking and listening.

She looked at all the horses, she listened to their neighs, the sounds of the birds, the rustle of the eucalyptus leaves and the murmur of the old dried grass that had seen last spring and summer, and the winter too, for Yarran knew that there were secrets she might learn.

Before she had been there long she could tell that the horses were restless as though expecting something, and the sounds in the grass and the leaves told her of something that had to be and would happen soon. Down here, too, low on the Tumut, the old bush legend of the vanishing sun, and of the union of

121

sun and moon, was being whispered ceaselessly.

Then she saw Ilinga's hoofmark.

Yarran stopped dead. She had not ever thought that Ilinga had come this way for the winter, but she would know her foster daughter's track among a million other tracks. It took very little seeking to find a full set of hoofmarks – another and another – and thus learn the way Ilinga had gone.

Scent still hung. It was not very long since Ilinga had headed upwards for the higher mountains. It was also not very long till Yarran discovered that a stallion had followed Ilinga, and that his tracks were made much more recently.

Yarran took a last, long, careful look at the big valley, eyes searching till she was quite certain that Ilinga had not returned to the horses by some other way. Then she set off to follow Ilinga's track, trotting along whenever the country allowed. The stallion's tracks showed that he was trotting too. Ilinga had only walked most of the time.

The day was already getting late. Night would come before she had gone very far, and though she would be able to follow scent, tracking by night would not be easy. Yarran kept going until dark, and then started off as moonlight sent cold fingers of light into the forest.

She kept thinking that the stallion's scent was so fresh that she must catch up with him soon, but she caught no sight nor sound of him. When the moon set, she rested again, and went on in the early-morning light.

From a rise on the ridge which she was travelling, about mid-day, Yarran saw through the trees that there was thick forest ahead, and then a sunlit clearing. It looked warm and bright, but there was no horse in it.

She trotted quite smartly through the open trees, and then had to slow down where the forest was thicker. She emerged into the clear country, the sunlit glade, and shivered because everything had got darker.

The tracks led right on. Ilinga's track showed she had trotted here, where the ground was not steep and rough. The stallion had trotted too. His scent was very fresh. Yarran

122

thought she might catch up with him. It was then that she also realized that she had been noticing for sometime the furtive, scuttling noises in the forest, and that now there were some kangaroos going very fast across the top of the glade.

Surely it was a little darker. She wondered where the kangaroos had vanished. Queer how there was no bird song, and now she could not hear the scuttling and rustling. She seemed to be alone. Suddenly she noticed how oppressive the day felt. She was getting very hot. She trotted on. 'Now, now, now, now,' was in the sound of her hoofbeats, in the beat of her pulse, as the heat and tension of the day mounted.

There was a band of white snow ahead. She would be able to roll to cool herself. When she reached it, it looked less shining white. She did not stop. Ilinga had crossed it, so had the unknown stallion. The snow was softening fast. The scent hung on the bushes and earth on the other side of it.

Yarran paused and sniffed. Ilinga's scent was as fresh as the stallion's now. Neither of them were very far ahead, and both were hurrying — she had been hurrying herself. Ilinga's scent was stronger, as though she were becoming afraid.

Had the day really got darker? Why was it so terribly quiet? Yarran hurried on, growing anxious, getting almost afraid herself.

The ridge rose up and up, and patches of snow became more frequent. Sometimes Yarran caught sight of much more snow ahead, but it had almost the look it gets as night comes ... a quietness ... so dark ...

Yarran pushed herself harder. She was beginning to get short of breath. That thick snow was not on the ridge which she was climbing. She realized that she had nearly reached the top of this ridge, and that it then continued on and on, and almost level.

Here, just on top of the ridge, the creek was below, on her off side. It was a large creek, and she saw that it must head further to the west, where the snow had been much heavier because the stream was very swollen.

She threaded her way through patches of snow, just as the

123

others ahead had done. Then she saw Ilinga in front, cantering, and a brown stallion following her, but they were like shadows, it had become so dark.

Dark, dark. They were all going into the dark. What had gone wrong with the day? It was surely only mid-day. Silence and oppressive heat - Yarran felt the sweat running off her coat. No other animals were about now. Ilinga was going faster and faster as though terror were after her – or ahead of her – and she was surely seeking Wurring. Dark, dark, was the sun vanishing?

Yarran stopped and looked up at the sky. All was dark. The lazy clouds were dark too. For one second before her eyes blinked, she saw through the fringe of her eyelashes a great shadow over the sun. She cast a quick look down to the creek, longing for a drink, noticed that logs and flood debris had caught together, damming it into a great, swirling pool in the narrow valley – dark water beneath the dark sky.

Yarran began to gallop after Ilinga. This must be what had been foretold. The sun would be almost extinguished – and Wurring was also the sun.

The sun was nearly gone. Yarran was getting closer and closer to the young stallion and he was not far behind Ilinga. The ridge had become narrow, and ahead there was a high, rough cliff. It looked as though it closed the valley. It loomed high in the darkness. Then she could hardly see even the cliff against the sky. Dark, dark, dark . . .

Yarran felt that she was galloping through the night, and some great menace was chasing her. It must have been the darkest moment – sometime back, when she stopped and looked up – because suddenly she knew that a little more light was creeping over the sky.

Ilinga must know where she was going. She was still moving so fast.

On and on they went, until they were almost beside that great, rearing cliff, and the two young ones ahead suddenly turned down the almost perpendicular drop into the valley. Yarran followed, and started to slide. She dug in her hooves to

124

stop herself.

As she looked up, the two vanished from her sight, one after the other – and it was getting much lighter, so they had not just gone into darkness.

Yarran went down carefully till, at her feet, the creek vanished into a large hole below the cliff. She took a step backwards in fright, then timidly stepped forward again, two or three steps, her nose timidly outstretched.

This was where Ilinga and the stallion had gone, for their scent was right to the edge, and so were their hoofmarks, slipping and sliding. But there was another scent too. Yarran sniffed eagerly.

It was quite fresh. Ilinga must have been going too fast, been too desperate to notice it.

Just on the other side of the creek was a hoofmark.

17: *Sun beneath a Shadow*

While the sun slowly and almost completely vanished beneath
a great, round shadow, Wurring and the iron-grey had fought
their way up the valley to the mouth of the cavern. There was

no mistaking the menace of the iron-grey. Both horses were terrified of the unnatural dark, and the older horse's terror had made him savage, determined to kill. Wurring could feel this, and suddenly knew that, even if the middle of the day had become dark and full of fear, if he were to live he must escape. If he stayed, death would claim him.

Behind was the tunnel into which Ilinga had disappeared. The tunnel would be dark anyway, whether it was dark or light outside. He would race up it, and away – if he could get away. He started to dance backwards into the cave, always facing the heavy stallion. The iron-grey followed. Maybe he would never get away from him, and the tunnel was so narrow it could give the stronger stallion a big advantage. He must try it – race beyond the boulders. Wurring swung around in the darkness and flicked his heels with great force as a parting kick at his opponent – and felt them strike flesh and bone very hard. There was no time to look back. He fled into the tunnel, and as fast as he could go along its smooth stone floor, deafened by the echoes of his own pounding hooves.

He remembered the boulders in time, and went slower. As the thundering, echoing noise died down, he realized that no one was following him. Perhaps that iron-grey had had enough of the tunnel, the time he chased Ilinga through it and was lamed. Wurring did not think of how his hooves had hit bone and flesh, but he did think that he must take care not to lame himself among the rocks. Then he felt the first line of boulders in front of him.

Wurring remembered those rocks. He remembered them as enormous, insurmountable boulders that had stopped him going with Ilinga, and he remembered it all in a queer haze, because he had been in great pain.

Now he was surprised to find that he could feel his way through them all fairly easily. Four good legs, of course, were better than three. He travelled quite quickly until he came to the very big boulder. Here he spent some time and had to search until he found the footholds around one side, and all that time there was no sound from the iron-grey.

Wurring got up on to the top of the rock, then he was over it, beyond it, and in the smooth tunnel again, hurrying. He came to the next lot of tumbled boulders and was almost over that before he felt the touch of fresh air on his face. There was no light because the sun had been almost extinguished, but as he reached the opening, there was certainly more light than there had been in the tunnel.

Wurring stood there, checked by the splashing water. How was he to get out?

Ilinga must have got out of here, so it must be possible. If only it were not so dark. Wurring was young and strong. He jumped on to the mud bank, which was smaller, now, because the water was continually splashing over it. From there he leapt straight up and out of the hole.

He stood for a moment, looking at the narrow valley, the great tall trees looming against the dark sky. Like Yarran, he saw through his eyelashes, for one fleeting second, that the sun was under a round cloud. Then he took a deep breath, filling his lungs.

The sun was almost extinguished, but he felt life and excitement surging through him. He turned his head towards Ravine and Numeramang, towards home, and he hoped, towards Ilinga, and he climbed, slithering and sliding, up the steep side of the valley.

He went fast because he had no wish to be caught again by the iron-grey, and the world was becoming slightly lighter. After a while he heard a sound far below him, and, thinking it was the iron-grey, he hurried even more. He must get up and out of this deep-cleft valley, out and away.

The light grew stronger. Once more daylight was coming back to the world as though there had been an unnatural and short night to break the rhythm of life. Wurring noticed that there were many more of the lazy clouds. It was very hot, too. The dripping sweat was not only caused by his speed and the fear he had felt.

He reached the top and could see great ridges and mountains of snow ahead. Then they were hidden under black cloud. Perhaps it had been raining up there for some time. Presently he felt the first huge spots falling on himself.

His way lay a little south of west, but that would lead him into the deepest snow, so he headed rather north of west, trying to get round most of the snow.

Sunlight fell between dense black clouds and illuminated the young horse with blazing light. Wurring reared up in the brightness. He felt wildly alive – and at last he was free and seeking Ilinga. Then it started to rain again.

Wurring kept on, trotting, cantering, picking his way between the heat-rotted fields of snow that were now visibly washing away. Even as he watched, rivulets formed everywhere and went tearing downwards.

The ground was slippery, was boggy, was very heavy going, but Wurring wanted to get as far away from that iron-grey as he could. At least this beating rain would wash away his tracks.

Rain on the back, rain in the eyes, water running down his shoulders – Wurring trotted on. Sometime, he knew, he would come to deep snow which might stop him.

The clouds lifted again, and he saw the mountains ahead. Maybe he would have to go even more northerly to find a way through – and now evening, real evening, was coming. There was no sound nor sign of anyone following. When night came he would be able to rest.

Sunlight fell obliquely, gliding banks of snow, shining on pools of water. Wurring's mane and tail were nearly dry. He shook himself so that the hairs separated, and suddenly he was sunlight, fire, life. Once he saw his shadow behind him on a field of snow, far bigger than life size.

The loneliness of the evening gripped him. Soon there would be no golden light, no glittering beams from between black clouds. A wild duck went winging across the snow, and there was the eerie cry of a plover from a bare swamp. The birds were as lonely as he, but they had started to move and call again, after that mid-day darkness. Lonely, lonely was the threnody of the plover, lonely the wild duck flying, neck outstretched.

129

Wurring was one horse alone, but he sought Ilinga, the filly who had come to Numeramang, that night of the full moon. It was not loneliness that she and her mother had brought with them – though death must be lonely – it was beauty and a strange dream of the future. A moonlight mare . . . Ilinga had a luminous quality in her coat – neither she nor her dam had had moonlight through their hair.

Wurring was tiring, and his head was in a cloud of old stories of the sun and the moon. The sun had vanished that day, of this he was certain. The brolgas had cried to the moon of great danger, and he had had danger enough. Now it was time to find Ilinga. Another wild duck flew high along a pale, blue-green rift in the sky.

Night was coming. Wurring began to look for some place that would be sheltered from the wind that was now turning cold.

There were rocks and some trees, some rather poor grass which he could nibble. He would camp there for the night. As he stopped moving, he thought he heard a distant neigh . . . a voice he knew? He did not like to answer because of the iron-grey, and the neigh – if it was one – did not sound again.

Wurring was very tired. He grazed for a while on the un-appetizing old grass, constantly looking up and all around. Then he backed himself against a tree in a cleft between rocks. He would sleep on his feet there, where no one could come at him from behind – but he did not sleep. He was tense, waiting for whatever the future held for him, the future that had been promised when that mare walked on to the Numeramang flat with the filly foal at foot, promised in that vibration which went through him as he touched the foal.

The moon rose and shone in Wurring's eyes. The moon had shone in that exhausted foal's eyes when she had opened them to look at him. Now Wurring was a grown horse, out alone in the snow and the moonlight, alone where the wind moaned through the rocks.

Did he hear that neigh again? No. Surely there was no sound except the wind. A fleeting picture of Yarran went through his mind, and he wondered where she was. Then he stretched himself, and knew he felt strong, wonderful.

Dawn came, and he set off again, hoping to get to Numer-amang that night, or at least to Ravine. It was possible that Ilinga had wintered at Ravine.

The night had turned very cold, so that the snow was more solid, that morning, and he walked over a gap between two higher hills, on the hard snow. The plain beyond was snow-covered, but woven over with the lines of open creeks. He would get across it somehow. He cantered down to it, bucking with joy.

The snow on the plain was still fairly firm. There, out on the white plain that was criss-crossed with cold blue creeks, the young chestnut horse galloped and played. Wurring had forgotten that there was any danger from the iron-grey, and danger left in the world, and he danced a dance that was only watched by a dingo and his mate, by the currawongs who flew high in the blue and silver sky, and a wedgetail eagle, planing higher still.

A faint, early breeze blew off the high mountains away in the south – its touch thrilling – and Wurring felt himself charged with tingling, burning fire. He swung around on his toes, reared and pranced. The dingo and his mate, the curra-wongs, and the eagle above saw beauty and grace, sunlight, and life's continuance in a chestnut horse, dancing, there, on the sunlit snow.

18: *The Sun, the Moon and the Snow*

Ilinga had not waited any longer, at that hole below the cliff, than it took to collect her feet beneath her and spring down. She was so terrified by the sun's disappearance, and so sure that it meant disaster for Wurring, that she hurtled herself over the boulders and down the tunnel. Even deeper darkness closed around her.

If she had not gone so fast, she would surely have picked up his scent. As it was, just once, when she paused to slide down the enormous boulder, she registered the scent of Wurring, but thought it was because she was so afraid for him that she could almost see him fighting the iron-grey, and so his scent had come to her nose, too.

Another reason to make her go faster and faster, was the young brown stallion. She had never expected him to jump into the tunnel after her. He was a fine horse, gentle and kind, but even the noise of one other horse could make any rescue of Wurring difficult. How, she wondered, how could she rescue Wurring, how, how, how?

As she neared the end of the tunnel, she forced herself to go slowly. Even with the stallion behind her, there was no sense in bursting out into the open. The sight of her might just make the iron-grey kill Wurring.

Ilinga suddenly felt desperate. Wurring and she had been together always, except for this last winter. They belonged together. He *must* be better now. He *must* be able to escape from the iron-grey, and go with her.

She walked very quietly towards the sandy cave. Why had there been no bats? Perhaps they had gone out because the sun

had vanished? She could not hear the brown stallion behind
her. She crept along the tunnel into the cave and – stopped,
just as her feet touched the sand.

Her hair stood up on end.

It was still only half light, outside, as the shadow passed off
the face of the sun, and in the half light Ilinga could see the
dark bulk of a horse lying right at the mouth of the cavern on

the sand. She could smell blood, and she could see a darker stain on the dark sand around that horse's head.

It was not Wurring's head, nor did that horse's body have the grace of Wurring's body. It was a heavy horse.

Ilinga had forgotten the brown stallion behind her. She crept closer to the horse that lay on the sand. She thought it was the iron-grey, and she had to be sure, and had to know whether he were alive or dead.

Closer, closer, she crept over the sand, and more and more light came into the sky.

The horse showed no sign of hearing her. His eyes were shut, but she could see a very slow, very faint rise and fall of his flanks with his breathing.

There was quite a lot of blood beneath his head, but, as the side that was damaged was underneath, she could not see what had happened. She stood close, looking down at him. The horse looked quite solid and very much alive. Death looked different from this. From a dead horse something had gone . . . breath . . . life . . . She stepped away, fast and silently, keeping watch on the horse and watch on the bush by the creek to which she was heading. She was almost certain that other eyes were watching from the black sallee trees.

If Wurring had been there, he would have come out to greet her. For a moment she stopped, one fore foot raised in the air: if it were not Wurring that had hurt the iron-grey, there would be another stallion in the trees somewhere. Rain was falling, but she did not notice it.

She could feel the eyes on her. Another stallion would have come out to see her too. She stood – nervous, fine-boned, beautiful filly, built for speed – and nothing stirred in the bush, but the eyes watched.

What was fear? She had to find Wurring, the sun. She moved quietly on towards those trees and over the creek. She heard a rumble of thunder. The rain drops bounced off her hot back, and she realized that it had been raining for some time. It was also slowly getting lighter.

Ilinga went through the creek very quietly, and up the high

bank on the further side. The eyes were retreating, silently retreating. Then suddenly there was the swish of branches. She could hear hooves stepping with care. Ilinga followed round the thick clump of black sallees. More trees were swishing. Whoever it was that had been there had gone into the next clump. They must have backed in, because Ilinga felt the eyes watching her again.

There could not be many horses, or there would be more noise, and she guessed they must be young ones – young fillies. There was no point in trying to catch them. All she wanted was Wurring, and she could see no sign of Wurring at all. She went down and crossed the creek again, to look for Wurring. The iron-grey was still lying in exactly the same position. She must hurry because it would be the end of everything if the iron-grey woke and caught her.

She was soon through the creek and back on the other side. The grassy flat stretched for some distance downstream. The grass was brown and pressed down by the weight of recent snow. She saw that a lot of it was churned up by horses' hooves.

She walked quickly, nose to ground, searching for clear tracks, trying to learn the story that all the marks would tell her, trying to pick up any scent that the rain had not already washed away. The earth was so churned that at first she could only learn that there had been horses fighting. She thought she heard more thunder, and began to search even more quickly. Milling marks were everywhere, then . . . there was a set of Wurring's hind hoofmarks, ground in as though he had reared to strike, and swivelled suddenly. There was also a fairly clear spoor of the iron-grey's.

Ilinga had learnt what she wanted to know, and unless any other horse had appeared, Wurring had knocked out the iron-grey and then vanished. He must have gone up the tunnel . . . his scent . . . she had not imagined it as she rushed down. Suddenly she wondered where that young brown stallion had got to – he had been close behind her and he had not appeared. Of course he had not known the way over some of the boulders,

135

and that could have slowed him up, or he might have turned back.

She looked up and saw the owners of the watching eyes quite clearly for a moment. They were standing as if turned to stone with terror, looking towards the cave. Ilinga froze. Had the iron-grey woken? But no, he was still lying there. Then she heard the sound of thunder again, and really took notice of it. Was it thunder, rumbling and roaring all around that cliff? It was not absolutely the same sort of sound as thunder . . . and it was becoming a rumbling roar . . . muffled.

Something dreadful was going to happen. Suddenly every instinct told her to go for her life on to high ground. She sprang through the creek and up the opposite bank. There was no time to be quiet or to keep hidden. Quick, quick! The sun had vanished, but it had returned: now something terrible was happening beneath that cliff.

She heard a horse's scream of terror. She stopped and looked at the cave. The iron-grey still lay there. Then out of the dark tunnel mouth, screaming with fear, galloped the young brown stallion. He was mad with fright. There was something behind him. It looked like a brown wall.

Ilinga saw him leap across the sand, past the unconscious iron-grey, and the wall seemed to burst behind him.

That wall was water – brown water that carried branches and logs – and it came so fast that the galloping stallion was caught by it, knocked over, hurtled into the creek.

Ilinga watched, but she scrambled upwards at the same time. She saw the brown stallion completely submerged, saw him bobbing up again, saw his head, realized his feet had found something solid on which to stand. She saw him balanced for one moment in the rushing brown water, then he leapt for the bank.

It was then that the iron-grey horse was lifted bodily by the great surge of water and tossed and swirled into the creek. There was no movement in him, other than the crazy movement caused by the water.

Part of the creek bank had been washed into the stream and

136

a leaning tree fell across the creek just as the wave of water carrying the iron-grey came down. The grey stallion hit the tree trunk: the flood water banked up behind for a few moments, but behind it still was the whole force of the dam that had been held away up the creek above the cliff, and this water broke over the iron-grey, and his body disappeared.

Ilinga did not see him again.

She saw the young brown stallion standing, trembling all over, his breath gasping, water dripping off him. She saw the two fillies, owners of those watching eyes, but now Ilinga had no other idea than to get to Wurring – and she was certain that Wurring had left the iron-grey and gone up that tunnel which was now full of water.

She stood watching. They all watched till at last the water started dropping. Ilinga knew that as soon as the stream had gone back to its ordinary size she must go up it and seek Wurring somewhere on the other side.

After a few moments the young stallion walked timidly over towards her, his eyes showing their whites each time he looked at the flood. She gave a little whinny to welcome him. Then the two fillies joined them. Further down the valley, a few rather troubled neighs rang out – a herd without a stallion, and nervous.

The four young animals stood together on the high ground while the water went down. A shaft of late sunshine fell through a gap in the hills on the western side, and through the black clouds. It illuminated the group just as Ilinga rubbed her head along the neck of the stallion, and then began to slip and slide her way down the muddy bank towards the cave and the tunnel.

For her there was no question of fear: there was only the idea of Wurring – the absolute compulsion to follow and to find him.

For the young brown stallion there was no question of ever going back through that tunnel again. He had saved his life by flinging himself off the high boulder and racing in front of the bow wave of damned-up water. In the tunnel there had been, for him, the sort of terror that no horse could face again.

Ilinga was going back up the tunnel. She looked at him once. He had followed and followed her, but she was sure he had known all along she was not for him. Here was a good valley, herd without a stallion and two beautiful fillies.

Ilinga entered the tunnel. For her there was no fear, only the necessity to find Wurring.

*   *   *

Ilinga's mind held no map of that tunnel now. Boulders had been rolled by the water as though they were thistle heads. There were logs wedged across the tunnel. There was a film of mud underfoot in some places, and scoured, slippery rock in others. Water dripped from the roof, and the sides were cold and wet – cold, so cold to touch the hot flanks or shoulders of the hurrying filly. Fear could not have turned her back, for she was seeking Wurring as though she were driven – but her nerves were so taut that a sudden onslaught of cold drips could force a horrified snort from her.

Darkness, darkness, danger. She wanted light – sunlight or moonlight – and Wurring.

She scrambled over the last boulders towards the patch of light. The hole into which the creek poured was far bigger now, and it was filled with logs and branches, Ilinga forced herself through all the debris and up out of the hole, and a wild neigh burst from her. Fear had been with her, after all, and now she called, though Wurring must surely be miles away.

A neigh answered her, dropping down into the valley from the high ridge above. Ilinga called again and again, and then started up, slithering crazily on the mud that coated the lower slopes.

It was Yarran who neighed up above – Yarran who had followed Wurring's track to the top of the ridge, and then seen the dammed-up waters in the valley burst and fill the hole into which Ilinga and the brown stallion had vanished.

138

Now there were the two mares going on over the mountains, aiming for Numeramang, if they could get there through the snow. Now it was not flood that was the danger, but that they should get caught in deep, heat-rotted snow, that they might plough on and on too far, and get too exhausted to get out.

Often they found a track of Wurring's to give them hope: then for miles there would be nothing. Wurring's gay, dancing tracks on the firm-frozen snow would have melted and vanished in the heat of the day.

Ilinga went on and on, and Yarran followed. It was Ilinga who was so powerfully drawn so that she could not rest. Somewhere there would be Wurring with sunlight setting his mane and forelock aflame.

*   *   *

It was night time, and Wurring had searched three days for Ilinga. She was not in Ravine where the grass was already spring-fresh. She was not in Numeramang, where some snow still lay in the shady places – where the everlastings that had once been golden and those that had been white let their brown seeds fly in the wind, whispering of a golden horse and a moonlight mare.

The currawongs, high in the bright, spring sky, told him, 'She seeks you. She seeks you.' The double warble of the red-tipped pardalottes who were hidden in the leaves of the snow-gums said: 'From the east: from the east.' The thrush's voice came as though through a melting snow crystal, with all the unbelievable beauty of the snow and the mountains – liquid, lovely, the joy of creation, and it told him that the moon would soon be full.

So Wurring went east, past Ravine again, and, as night fell, he slept in a valley between high ridges, and the snow still lay all around.

Yarran and Ilinga travelled that night, after the full moon had risen, and, when it was nearly morning, as the two mares

139

stepped with swinging strides over the frozen snow, there sounded a call over the long, white ridges. Yarran threw up her head and listened. This call was for her, not Ilinga, and she answered, but she went on with Ilinga, knowing that the horse who had called her would not be far away.

Then there was another call, and this time Ilinga's head went up in the air, and the moonlight ran through her mane and forelock, silver hair rippling.

Yarran stopped.

The moon was shining in their eyes now, soon it would set in the west. Then over the high, white ridge behind them came the first light from the sun. It only touched the high snow ridges that lay far ahead, beneath the full moon.

Yarran heard the stallion calling for her again. She turned and went.

A currawong soared high in the air calling: 'It is now: it is now,' and Ilinga went forward to meet Wurring, moonlight glinting on the silver hair in her mane and her tail and all the silver hairs that had come shining along her back in her spring coat, this year when she had grown to her full beauty.

Her moon shadow stretched out behind her, and Wurring's

140

was ahead of him on the moon-glittering snow. Closer and closer, the young horses cantered over the snow, frost crystals flying up from their hooves catching the silver light of the moon; Wurring's shadow racing ahead, pointing towards Il-inga, and all the time the sky grew lighter.

They were two or three strides apart when the sun came up over the snowy ridge. Ilinga's shadow leapt to meet Wurring, and his shadow was suddenly behind him – the two shadows flaring into a luminous, purple-blue in the blend of sunlight and moonlight. All the frost crystals which flew up from their hooves became luminous and blue also, and for the few minutes before the sun rose higher and while the moon still shone, the two young horses danced on the snow surrounded by snow-spray and shadows of a deep, transparent blue. For sunlight and moonlight had met over the glittering snow, in a strange light and a strange night, and the chestnut stallion danced, with the sunlight in his mane, and the mare was shining with the light of the moon.

ENID BLYTON is Dragon's bestselling author. Her books have sold millions of copies throughout the world and have delighted children of many nations. Here is a list of her books available in Dragon Books:

FIRST TERM AT MALORY TOWERS	30p	☐
SECOND FORM AT MALORY TOWERS	30p	☐
THIRD YEAR AT MALORY TOWERS	30p	☐
UPPER FOURTH AT MALORY TOWERS	30p	☐
IN THE FIFTH AT MALORY TOWERS	30p	☐
LAST TERM AT MALORY TOWERS	30p	☐
MALORY TOWERS GIFT SET	£1·20	☐
6 Books ENID BLYTON		
THE TWINS AT ST. CLARE'S	30p	☐
SUMMER TERM AT ST. CLARE'S	30p	☐
SECOND FORM AT ST. CLARE'S	30p	☐
CLAUDINE AT ST. CLARE'S	30p	☐
FIFTH FORMERS AT ST. CLARE'S	30p	☐
THE O'SULLIVAN TWINS	30p	☐
ST. CLARE'S GIFT SET	£1·00	☐
5 Books ENID BLYTON		
MYSTERY OF THE BANSHEE TOWERS	30p	☐
MYSTERY OF THE BURNT COTTAGE	30p	☐
MYSTERY OF THE DISAPPEARING CAT	30p	☐
MYSTERY OF THE HIDDEN HOUSE	30p	☐
MYSTERY OF HOLLY LANE	30p	☐
MYSTERY OF THE INVISIBLE THIEF	30p	☐
MYSTERY OF THE MISSING MAN	30p	☐
MYSTERY OF THE MISSING NECKLACE	30p	☐
MYSTERY OF THE PANTOMIME CAT	30p	☐
MYSTERY OF THE SECRET ROOM	30p	☐
MYSTERY OF THE SPITEFUL LETTERS	30p	☐
MYSTERY OF THE STRANGE BUNDLE	30p	☐
MYSTERY OF THE STRANGE MESSAGES	30p	☐
MYSTERY OF TALLY-HO COTTAGE	30p	☐
MYSTERY OF THE VANISHED PRINCE	30p	☐
TALES FROM THE BIBLE	30p	☐
CHILDREN'S LIFE OF CHRIST	30p	☐
THE BOY WHO TURNED INTO AN ENGINE	30p	☐
THE BOOK OF NAUGHTY CHILDREN	30p	☐
A SECOND BOOK OF NAUGHTY CHILDREN	30p	☐

PONY BOOKS are very popular with boys and girls.
Dragon Books have a fine selection by the best authors to choose from:

SPECIAL DELIVERY	Gillian Baxter	17p ☐
PANTOMIME PONIES	Gillian Baxter	17p ☐
SILVER BRUMBY'S KINGDOM	Elyne Mitchell	30p ☐
SILVER BRUMBIES OF THE SOUTH		
	Elyne Mitchell	30p ☐
SILVER BRUMBY	Elyne Mitchell	30p ☐
SILVER BRUMBY'S DAUGHTER	Elyne Mitchell	30p ☐
MY FRIEND FLICKA PART 1	Mary O'Hara	30p ☐
MY FRIEND FLICKA PART 2	Mary O'Hara	30p ☐
GREEN GRASS OF WYOMING 1	Mary O'Hara	25p ☐
GREEN GRASS OF WYOMING 2	Mary O'Hara	25p ☐
GREEN GRASS OF WYOMING 3	Mary O'Hara	25p ☐
THUNDERHEAD 1	Mary O'Hara	25p ☐
THUNDERHEAD 2	Mary O'Hara	25p ☐
THUNDERHEAD 3	Mary O'Hara	25p ☐
FOR WANT OF A SADDLE		
	Christine Pullein-Thompson	20p ☐
IMPOSSIBLE HORSE	Christine Pullein-Thompson	20p ☐
THE SECOND MOUNT	Christine Pullein-Thompson	25p ☐
THE EMPTY FIELD	Christine Pullein-Thompson	25p ☐
THREE TO RIDE	Christine Pullein-Thompson	25p ☐
THE PONY DOPERS	Christine Pullein-Thompson	25p ☐
A SWISS ADVENTURE	Pat Smythe	20p ☐
A SPANISH ADVENTURE	Pat Smythe	20p ☐

All these books are available at your local bookshop or newsagent, or can be ordered direct from the publisher. Just tick the titles you want and fill in the form below.

Name ....

Address ....

Write to Dragon Cash Sales, PO Box 11, Falmouth, Cornwall TR10 9EN

Please enclose remittance to the value of the cover price plus:

UK: 18p for the first book plus 8p per copy for each additional book ordered to a maximum charge of 66p

BFPO and EIRE: 18p for the first book plus 8p per copy for the next 6 books, thereafter 3p per book

OVERSEAS: 20p for first book and 10p for each additional book

Granada Publishing reserve the right to show new retail prices on covers, which may differ from those previously advertised in the text or elsewhere.